"There're two men outside. One has a gun."

"What are they doing?" Liam palmed his cell phone. He didn't have his service weapon on him.

Thankfully, Blake had her gun in the closet safe.

"I can't tell who they are," Blake said, "but it feels like they're waiting. Take this and go look for yourself." She handed the gun to him. "You can see them if you look outside of the kitchen window."

Liam made it to the kitchen. He could see the men clearly from the window.

Just as Blake described, there were two of them standing at the edge of the yard.

Liam did some quick mental math. Instead of calling the sheriff's department, he called Price, who was closer.

"I'm at Blake's house and there are two men standing outside. One is armed. I can't tell about the other. Me, Blake, Lola and the kids are in here. We have only one gun between us."

"That's the back door," Blake said. "Someone's trying to come in."

SEARCH FOR THE TRUTH

TYLER ANNE SNELL

INTRIGUE

This book is for Danielle Haas. If I could insert a ten-minute voice memo here, I would. Instead I'll just say this book exists simply because you're a wonderful friend. Thank you for always being there.

Harlequin®
INTRIGUE™

Recycling programs for this product may not exist in your area.

ISBN-13: 978-1-335-45731-8

Search for the Truth

Copyright © 2025 by Tyler Anne Snell

Harlequin Enterprises ULC
22 Adelaide St. West, 41st Floor
Toronto, Ontario M5H 4E3, Canada
www.Harlequin.com

Printed in U.S.A.

Tyler Anne Snell lives in South Alabama with her same-named husband, their artist kiddo, four mini "lions" and a burning desire to meet Kurt Russell. Her superpowers include binge-watching TV and herding cats. When she isn't writing thrilling mysteries and romance, she's reading everything she can get her hands on. How she gets through each day starts and ends with a big cup of coffee. Visit her at www.tylerannesnell.com.

Books by Tyler Anne Snell

Harlequin Intrigue

Manhunt
Toxin Alert
Dangerous Recall

Small Town Last Stand

Search for the Truth

The Saving Kelby Creek Series

Uncovering Small Town Secrets
Searching for Evidence
Surviving the Truth
Accidental Amnesia
Cold Case Captive
Retracing the Investigation

Winding Road Redemption

Reining in Trouble
Credible Alibi
Identical Threat
Last Stand Sheriff

Visit the Author Profile page at Harlequin.com.

CAST OF CHARACTERS

Liam Weaver—Becoming sheriff didn't stop this veteran from his plan to live a quiet life. However, taking on a closed case that leads him right to a woman who has the entire town talking, he realizes there's only one plan left—leave his calm for her chaos.

Blake Bennet—Returning to her hometown and leaving her career behind was never in Sheriff Trouble's cards. Yet raising her late sister's children becomes her only focus. That is, until a suspicious case pulls her toward a man who will do everything to protect her and the only family she has left.

Missy Clearwater—The well-known daughter of an important Seven Roads business owner. The investigation into her death pits the entire town against the sheriff.

Price Collins—Deputy with the sheriff's department, this career local stays loyal to the current sheriff and Sheriff Trouble as the stakes rise higher.

Lola Bennet—Stepmother to Blake, she moves in to help raise four-year-old Clementine and baby Bruce.

Beth Bennet—Her death changed Blake's future, but her past might be the key to solving the mysteries plaguing the town.

Ryan Reed—As Blake's former brother-in-law, his sudden appearance in Seven Roads raises several red flags and questions.

Prologue

The locals of Seven Roads, Georgia, were all saying the same thing. Missy Clearwater went and jumped off the old, haunted bridge near Becker Farm because she was mighty unhappy with her father, her ex and the fact that her best friend had taken all but two seconds to hook up with that same ex a week before.

It was a sad piece of news that traveled across the small, action-deprived town with breakneck speed. Starting with Abe Becker and his son, who had found her. Both of whom were still upset about it all, only for different reasons.

"Sheriff, I feel for the girl, I really do, but who's goin' to fix the damage she left behind?" Abe asked, thumbs hooked around his overall loops. He was nearing seventy, but the way he kept doing chores on his land would have made you double-check that math.

Liam Weaver, said sheriff, envied the man a little. He was in his thirties and was already fighting with a hip that locked up and ached if he skipped out on his physical therapy. Something he'd been lax about the last few weeks. The weather wasn't helping. It had been a surprisingly dreary and cold month. He tried to actively not favor his side and instead readjusted his belt, skimming his badge in the process. The metal was cold against his hand. Abe was a contrast with his reddening face.

"Are you talking about the wooden board that broke?" Liam had to ask to be sure. "The one that most likely gave way before she fell?"

Abe was a nodding mess.

"That bridge may be old, but it's still on my property," he said. "Not fixing it isn't an option for me."

Liam shared a quick look with Abe's son, Junior. He was closer to Liam's age and looked mighty ashamed.

"Dad, it was only one board," he tried. "We can fix it later."

Abe shooed the thought off with two in-sync and annoyed hand gestures.

"That's what I'm getting at." He motioned behind him where the great majority of his acreage sat. "Every penny counts in this place. Every single one has a purpose and a job. We take that money from somewhere it's needed and put it somewhere that it ain't, and we'll have problems. Problems I'm not paying for."

The last part was directed at Liam.

He tried to maintain an air of professionalism.

It was hard. His response was blunt.

"Well, Miss Clearwater can't pay for it, Abe, and I'll be honest. I'm not about to ask her parents for it while they're planning a funeral."

Junior's shame doubled in on itself, lining his face with a frown that sunk farther than a stone in water.

His daddy, at least, seemed to feel some of the ripples.

Abe let out a breath that was all frustration. He shook his head.

"I suppose I shouldn't go doing that right now," he relented. "Maybe it's something we can talk about down the line."

Junior saw his opportunity. He took his dad's shoulders and turned him away from the woods they were standing near.

"Until then we should leave the sheriff and deputies to do what it is they need to do." Junior nodded deep to Liam. "Y'all have our permission to come and go as you see fit until all of this gets settled. If you need anything, you know where to find us."

Abe looked like he wanted to gripe about that, but his son was faster. Liam only got one nod in before the two were back in their work truck and driving back the way they had come.

It left Liam with an ache in his hip but some contentedness in his chest.

He liked the silence that being alone brought.

That silence didn't last long.

Deputy Perry "Price" Collins got out of his cruiser rolling his eyes.

"Sorry to leave you hanging there, Sheriff," he said. "But I've spent almost all my life avoiding Old Man Becker ever since he caught me and my girlfriend hooking up in his barn in high school. That man not only tore into my hide for trespassing, he also *saw* my bare hide while he was doing it." Price shook his head. "That whole incident is why I learned to put my britches on faster than a lightning strike after that."

Liam liked the quiet, but of the constant noises in his work life, Price was one he disliked the least. For the past two years he had been more of a right-hand man than anyone else in the small-as-a-thimble McCoy County Sheriff's Department. He had also been the one who most respected privacy when it came to after-work hours. While they saw each other almost every day, they seldom spoke outside of the office.

"I've heard that story three times now, and I still don't know why you'd pick a barn to do that in. Especially on the Becker land. There had to be a better place."

Price snorted. "Believe me, that's the best we had at the time. My cousin Dwayne tried the whole parking-in-the-middle-of-nowhere thing and somehow had the entire law banging on his Ford's windows before the clock even struck nine." He shook his head again. "Give me Old Man Becker and him raising his voice at me over seeing someone with a badge holding a flashlight outside of my car door any day."

Liam wasn't sure which option was worse to him and decided it wasn't the time to get into it. Not with what they had to do next. He glanced up at the darkening sky and felt the wind try to bite into his jeans. It was only a matter of time before the rain came in and made things more difficult. A sentiment that Price seemed to agree with. He dropped his humor and secured his flashlight at his side.

"Ready when you are, boss."

The Becker Farm was the largest piece of acreage owned by a resident in the entirety of Seven Roads. The woods that took up the back end felt just as expansive. Once inside the tree line and it felt like another world.

A world that all the teens of Seven Roads at some point tried to sneak through to get to the bridge.

Stretching across one of the only major drop-offs on the property, the bridge stood over what used to be a deep creek. That creek had long since dried out. Which made the drop from the worn wood above so deadly.

Ten minutes later and Liam stopped just outside of the first plank with a sigh that pulled all of him down.

"Did you know Missy?" he asked when Price stopped next to him.

The younger man was quick to nod.

"I met her at a few birthday parties that my daughter, Winnie, went to when she was younger. Though Missy was there as friends of the older siblings since there was an age difference. I'm more familiar with her father."

That wasn't a surprise considering Jonathan Clearwater had run the tractor auction and supply business that had employed close to fifty people in town before he had sold it off, something that had happened way before Liam's time in town but that he'd heard about still. Seven Roads had less than one thousand residents. Things like fifty jobs leaving town was a big deal, even after the fact.

"It gives me a cold stomach thinking about it," Price added on. "Death is sad enough. Add in the fact that I have a picture with Missy and my little girl enjoying a birthday party at the arcade, and it hits different, you know?"

Liam didn't dispute that.

He did, however, get down to business.

"Let's go ahead and take the pictures Doc Ernest is asking for. You want the high ground or low?"

Price was quick.

"High." Liam's eyebrow went up at that. Price explained with a small smile. "Old Man Becker might have caught me full moon in his barn, but there isn't a kid who grew up in Seven Roads who hasn't navigated this bridge a hundred times at least. I know all the soft, squeaky parts. It'll be safer if I take the pictures up here. Trust me."

Liam snorted.

"You locals sure know how to party."

Price shrugged.

"Not all of us could be so cool as to grow up in a city. Us country folk had to make do."

Price pulled out his phone and was off. Liam took a beat before he took the path to the left. It led down a slope that hurt his hip but wasn't all that unmanageable otherwise. A few careful feet later and he was at the flat rock and dirt-covered ground beneath the bridge. It was an odd feeling being there again. He'd been the first one to arrive after the call was made, and while he'd seen horrible things during his deployments, seeing Missy had been different.

A young woman who had been pushed around so much that she'd found herself over the edge.

Cases like this never got easier.

Liam took out his phone and started snapping pictures of the area. Their medical examiner had asked for more pictures of the scene after the area had been cleared. He wasn't sure why, but he trusted that the good doctor had a reason.

So that's what Liam did for the next few minutes. He walked the area around and beneath the bridge, mindful of the details.

That's when he saw it.

Partially buried in the dirt, blending in next to some rocks. A slight shine to it, dirty silver.

On reflex Liam pulled out the pair of gloves he always had on him during work. He put them on and picked up the small object.

It was a USB drive. There were no markings on it, but there were two letters written in marker on one side.

"M.C.," he read out loud.

Missy Clearwater?

Liam turned the drive over again, then scanned the area once more.

His phone started to vibrate in his hand. Doc Ernest's name was on the screen.

"Hey, Sheriff, are you still at the scene?" she asked instead of a greeting.

There was a rush to her words. An urgency.

Liam's gut started grumbling.

"I am. We're finishing up with the pictures. What's up?"

There was movement on her side of the phone. When she spoke again, she was nearly whispering.

"I'm going to need you to take a lot more pictures. And do a dang good job of it."

Liam wanted to say he always gave the job his best, but something in her tone pulled a question out of him instead.

"What's up?"

There was hesitation.

But then there was certainty.

"Because I think Missy Clearwater might have already been dead before she hit the ground."

Chapter One

Blake Bennet had been to many crime scenes over the last ten years or so. It had come with the territory of being law enforcement, never mind the fact that she'd been a sheriff for many of those years. But her reign with a badge had ended and, she thought, with it any sense of being amid the chaotic aftermath of someone's life again.

Boy had she been wrong.

Currently her living room would have given the crime scene unit a run for their money.

"Blake! We're going to be late." A woman, brightly dressed but frowning severely, hurried into the room with bangles clanking and a baby on her hip squirming. In the last six months of sharing a home with her stepmother, Blake was still getting used to her jack-in-the-box sudden appearances around their house.

That went double for the toddler and baby who had managed to turn the room into a disaster movie within the blink of an eye.

"I can't find the keys," Blake yelled right back. "And unless you've learned how to fly in the last ten minutes, we need those to get going."

Lola had not in fact learned how to fly in the last ten minutes.

She balanced Bruce on her hip and started throwing couch cushions and blankets around while Blake went back to her grid patterned search. Once she had been searching for a man buried alive and yet, somehow, the pressure she felt now was really grating. It didn't help that she already knew what would happen when they got to the school gym.

Everyone in Seven Roads would look at her.

The absent aunt come back home to take on the job title of inexperienced mother. Add in the fact that she was single, technically unemployed and living under the same roof with the stepmother she had barely known before coming back, and Blake was a walking, talking tabloid story for the town.

The gutsy Seven Roads locals would talk to her—the rest would talk in whispers.

It was, at best, annoying. At worst, it just plain hurt.

"Blake!" Lola exclaimed, pulling her attention with a start. She was pointing across the room to the one calm thing among the chaos. "Clem has them in her hand!"

Clementine Bennet was a quiet four. While her baby brother and her stepgrandma were expressive creatures, Clem was an observer first, a toddler second. Blake was reminded of the demeanor of the detectives she had worked with during her tenure in law enforcement. Watch people, take in the details and then communicate when necessary, if at all.

"Good girl, Clem," Blake said, relief washing over her. "Now let's get moving!"

That relief lasted for the time it took to get from the house to the Seven Roads High School's main gym. Since the town had limited space, any and every big event had been held in the same building since even before Blake had been a student there. Now in her thirties, it felt odd enough to park in the same lot she had when she was sixteen. It was a sentiment that she didn't have the luxury to let linger too long.

The second she had Clem out of her car seat, the child decided to become a world-class soccer player. Without a ball she made do with her shoes. One hit the floorboard, the other soared over Blake's shoulder like she had it headed straight for the game-winning goal.

"Forget the shoe," Lola said, hustling around. "Here, you take Bruce, I'll get Clem backstage, and you get us a seat. I already let Janie know we're heading in, so she's waiting at the door."

Blake was used to giving orders, but she had been finding that since moving back to her hometown, listening to Lola had become second nature. So she did as she was told. They switched kids and both sprinted off in different directions. Bruce squealed in delight at the rush. Blake just hoped there were seats available since they were downright late.

The gym lobby had a handmade banner that read Brightwell Daycare: What We Learned stretched over the three sets of double doors. Only two people were inside the lobby, but neither paid attention to Blake as she hurried to the doors. She peered through the glass and let out a breath.

The stage was empty.

The show hadn't started.

They still had time to grab some seats and maybe avoid people even noticing she was there.

She put her free hand on the door, ready to go inside, when that hope was dashed.

"Blake Bennet?"

One of the two other people in the lobby was now standing at her side. It had been years since Blake had been back to Seven Roads for any real length of time, and yet she recognized the woman instantly.

Corrie Daniels.

Blake would have preferred being trapped in an interrogation room with a feral tiger than talk with Corrie "Gossip Queen" Daniels.

But since that wasn't an option, Blake pulled her fake smile on tight.

"Hey there, Corrie. It's been a while."

"It has!" she exclaimed before letting out a trill of unnecessary laughter. She motioned to the front doors behind them. "I had to do a double take when I saw you. I mean, I heard you were back, but I guess seeing is believing, you know?"

Her gaze fell to Bruce.

Blake knew where this was going, and she wanted to nip it in the bud.

She made sure her smile stayed on and did her own little laugh.

"Actually, do you mind if we catch up later?" Blake asked. "Clem is in the program and we're running a bit late, so I still need to get some seats."

Corrie's entire expression fell into one of immense pity. Blake knew the look well by now. She had been getting it since her sister Beth's funeral. Never mind when word had gotten out that Blake would be raising her children. That pity seemed to split between the children losing their mother, Beth losing her life and Blake stumbling into a new reality she had never prepared for.

Blake had to hand it to Corrie though. While a lot of people tried to pretend that life had gone exactly the way they had planned it to, Corrie didn't even bother putting on airs. Why walk on eggshells when you only care about eating the omelet?

She reached out and patted Blake's shoulder.

"You come see me when you have the time," she cooed. "I know all of this must be so hard on you. I don't even know if I could do it. Never mind by myself. Poor thing."

Fake words. Fake concern. Fake pity.

Blake despised it.

Blake felt the strength behind her smile waver.

Anger was starting to claw its way up instead.

Thankfully, her personal jack-in-the-box popped up just in time.

"I suggest we save the chatter for later," Lola said, stopping at Blake's side. She nodded to Corrie. "You better go on in and find your seat. We'll be in right on after."

Corrie's mask of sympathy didn't slip, but she conceded with a nod. The hand already on Blake's shoulder squeezed once.

"Hang in there," she said. Then she did what Corrie did best. The perfect parting shot, the multitooled weapon of the South. "Bless your heart."

Blake's hand clenched into a fist at her side, but Corrie was already through the doors. She expected Lola to follow, but instead the older woman hung back.

It wasn't for support.

Lola turned Blake around to face her.

"I know you're probably getting near overwhelmed today, but I have to tell you something you're not going to like." Her expression softened. Blake couldn't help but brace herself.

Then Lola sighed out big.

"Bruce spit up."

Together they looked down at Blake's chest. Sure enough from her shoulder, down the yellow print on her dress, was baby Bruce spit up. She must have been more tired than she original thought. She hadn't even felt it.

"The one time I wear a dress," Blake breathed out.

Lola reached out for Bruce and laughed.

"The bathroom is around the corner. Hurry up and clean that so you're not smelling it the whole time. I'll get us seats."

So Lola took Bruce, and Blake was off and speed-walking to the same bathroom she had used countless times as a teen. She went to the task at hand with the same urgency, thinking about how she should have packed the towel parents used in this sort of situation.

She pictured it sitting on the dining room table.

Blake sighed again.

Her gaze shifted up to her reflection in the mirror.

Before six months ago she had always styled her hair into one long braid. Part habit, part utility. One single braid that always rested against her back. Contained. In order. Familiar.

Now her hair was down and short, a choice she had made to save time. To save energy.

But seeing herself now, seeing the bags under her eyes and the frown across her lips, the question that often bothered her came right on back.

If she couldn't take care of something simple like her hair, how could she take care of two little humans?

The ache in her chest grew cold.

It started to spread.

Blake shook her head.

"Now's not the time," she told herself. She straightened her dress and eyed the spot where the spit-up had been. She'd worn the wrong color of dress. The water stain was more than noticeable.

It made her grumble as she left the bathroom and hurried back to the lobby doors. Logically, she knew that no one would really care about it. That it wasn't a big deal. Yet, she hesitated before going inside.

Blake knew that it wasn't about the stain.

It was about the people.

And that made her feel shame.

She had dealt with all kinds of life-and-death situations,

and here she was worried about gossip from people she had known all of her life.

On reflex her hand clenched again.

It was only by the grace of luck that she didn't use her fist when a man came up at her side and startled her.

"Excuse me."

The voice was a deep, deep baritone. A sound that almost felt like it was anchoring her to the spot. Which seemed to match perfectly with the man it had come from.

He was tall. A tall that would have been comical on most, yet the man was wearing his height, and everything else, well. He looked tailor-made by a group of women who had grown up watching romance movies, where the male lead was the rough-and-tumble handyman next door. Dark eyes, dark hair slightly unruly but in a neat way, facial hair clipped close, and all pleasing angles making up a face that was as handsome as it was alarming when it popped up out of nowhere. There was a scar, she thought, near his neck, but for the life of her, Blake's detail-oriented brain skittered a bit.

The best she could do was raise an eyebrow in question.

A question that the man answered before she could put it into words.

"I thought maybe this could help you out for the time being." He held out a denim shirt. Blake was so flustered she took it. The man nodded to the doors. "It might make you more comfortable in there."

Blake blinked a few times.

"You want me to wear this?"

The man shrugged.

"If you want to, you can. I've seen a few ladies come in wearing these things like jackets, so it might look trendy."

Blake was about to do the polite thing and refuse the offer, but feedback from the gym cut through the thought. Blake turned toward the window on the door. The daycare director was at the microphone onstage.

"If you don't want to wear it, it's no big deal," the man added. "You can just throw it on the chair over there."

He pointed to the corner of the lobby.

Blake eyed the shirt in her hands.

It was long-sleeved and blue. A button-up left open. It seemed clean enough and would certainly cover the water stain.

The man went through the doors without another word.

Blake opened her mouth to tell him no thanks, ask his name and ask why he was doing this, but the director's voice cut off all worries.

Blake put the shirt on like a jacket and hurried inside.

LIAM FOUND THE woman when a little girl onstage told the entire gym about the differences between moths and butterflies. While the girl was quiet and mostly still, a woman in the last row of seating was not. She shot up tall and wielding two cell phones, both of which were trained squarely on the kid. From Liam's angle, he could see her mouthing along with the short speech.

He could also she was wearing his shirt.

Liam was glad for it. Offering the piece of clothing to her had been an impulsive act. One that had been spurred on by her body language alone.

He hadn't meant to, but Liam watched as she tensed and panicked, as she balled her hands into fists, as she hesitated.

All while outside of a daycare program.

Liam had thought about his own mother when he was a kid. She'd had to do a lot solo since his father was deployed. Liam didn't know this woman's story—if she was single or if she was temporarily by herself—but the urge to help her had been one he couldn't ignore. He had only hoped it would be helpful.

He was glad to see that it must have been.

"Hey, I found her." Price sidled up to him, voice low. They were standing at the wall on the side of the open gym. The lights were mostly off, so the stage was the center of attention, but Liam could still see where Price pointed.

"She's in the flowery dress with the big hair," he added on.

Liam nodded and pushed his arm back down.

It was bad enough he'd had to come out to the daycare program to track down a potential lead, but then again, it wasn't like Cassandra West had given them many choices.

"Make sure you're casual about your run-in with her, or she's going to feel like we ambushed her," Price said, once again. "Cass might not be as popular as she once was, but tick her off, and it'll be like kicking a hornet's nest."

"I'm not here to ambush her," Liam defended. "I'm here to make an appointment, is all. It's not a big deal."

That was a lie. It was a big deal to Liam.

Cassandra was one of the last people to see Missy Clearwater alive.

It had been more than two months since Missy's body had been found. In the time since, her case had been ruled a suicide. It was a point of severe contention between Liam and the general public. Everyone had believed that Missy's life had taken such a turn that her ending had made sense. There was no hard evidence to say otherwise, and even her own flesh and blood had accepted this tragic outcome. Doc Ernest's original suspicion had also changed. Like Price, she had had an emotional reaction to the death of a woman she had watched grow up. So much so, she had mistaken a hope that Missy hadn't done it to herself for a gut instinct that someone had been behind it.

When, in reality, the fall had been what had done the girl in.

That should have been that, but Liam… He couldn't let it go.

He hadn't watched Missy Clearwater grow up, but his gut had doubled down on something not being quite right.

And that all started from the flash drive he had found beneath the bridge.

That's why, months later, he was still trying to piece together the day of Missy's death. Off the books. For his own peace of mind.

It's why he needed to talk to Cassandra West.

And if that meant starting that talk off casually, then he would.

Ten minutes later and that need was bristling under Liam's skin. He wasn't a man who fidgeted, but the urgency had him out of the gym and standing in the parking lot before the waves of people started to filter out.

However, he bumped into someone else first.

"Here."

Liam looked down at the woman who had tapped his shoulder. Red hair, green eyes and a pretty sun dress with a spit-up stain on it.

She smiled. She was holding his shirt.

"Thank you for this," she added. "It saved me from freezing under that AC for sure. I hope you weren't too cold."

Liam, not a man built for small talk, found an easy smile. He tapped his short sleeve.

"No worries here. I'm built warm."

Liam was about to ask where her kids were, genuinely curious, but the woman's gaze went behind him in the parking lot. With it, her smile disappeared.

Tension lined every inch of her so quickly that Liam's body mirrored that tension on reflex.

It was such a complete change that Liam was about to ask what was wrong, but the woman was faster than his concern.

She pressed his shirt into his chest.

"Thanks again," she said, words cold. "If you'll excuse me."

Liam turned around to watch the woman walk with purpose toward something else.

Someone else.

A man he didn't recognize was standing at the end of the parking lot, staring.

And it wasn't until the woman got closer to him that he turned tail and ran into the wooded area behind the school. And it wasn't until he was running that the woman gave chase, disappearing into the tree line in a flash.

And it wasn't until that moment that Liam forgot all about his potential lead.

He was off and running into the woods right after them, nothing but red hair in his mind.

Chapter Two

It had been years since Blake had been in the woods behind the high school. Set between the gym's parking lot and the old building that had housed a Kmart half a mile away, between the trees had become just another rite of passage for Seven Roads' teens.

They couldn't escape the boredom of small-town life; they could skip a few of their classes though.

Now Blake didn't see how she had navigated the area as carefree as she had back then. A few feet in and a tree root nearly took her down. She caught her balance halfway through the fall. Her dress wasn't as fortunate. She heard the tear but didn't stop to investigate.

Instead, she was all eyes on Ryan Reed.

"Stop running," she yelled out to him, rounding another tree he had tried to put between them.

Ryan had never been the fastest kid in school, but as an adult, he had seemed to inherit a talent for being slippery. He wove through the underbrush and oaks like the snake that he was.

Too bad for him that Blake had made a career out of having faster reflexes than most of the people she ended up chasing.

Instead of running behind him directly, Blake cut to the

right and picked up speed. If her memory wasn't that far off, there was a slight hill that sloped up before sliding down into a small clearing. She could make up some space and cut him off.

So Blake followed her plan with total dedication. She didn't stop when she got tripped up again, she didn't stop when a low-hanging branch scratched at her face, and she didn't let up even an inch when her legs burned as she ran up and then down the small hill into the clearing.

She only stopped once she realized her plan had worked.

Ryan was holding his side and gasping. He broke through the tree line like he'd run a marathon. Blake closed the distance between them before Ryan realized she had cut him off.

His eyes widened.

Blake held out her hands in a stop motion.

"What are you—"

Before she could finish the question, Ryan did something Blake truly didn't expect.

He lunged at her.

Years of experience sang to her muscles. Instead of trying to avoid the hit, her legs and core braced themselves as her hands worked in sync while serving two different purposes.

Blake's left hand jabbed up in time to grab his wrist opposite her. Her right hand turned into a fist.

A fist that was angry.

It connected against the unsuspecting Ryan with enough power to throw him off his game. He stumbled to the side, only held up by her grip. Blake wasn't a petite woman, but Ryan still had some height on her. He lost his footing for a moment only to turn in the next and strike out with his free hand again.

It wasn't his fist that hit Blake but his elbow.

She cried out as pain exploded in her eyebrow.

Instead of trying to keep up with him, Blake decided to create some distance. She let go of his wrist and pivoted away.

"Stop this," she ground out.

Blake took a step back to try to meet his eye.

Ryan had both his fists up. Blake had only one ready. She knew what she was capable of and that she could do some damage. But that didn't mean she wanted to go against him again.

"What are you doing?" she tried. "Why did you run?"

Ryan's face was turning red. He shook his head with obvious aggression.

"Just tell me where it is," he spat. "I know you're—you're working on it."

Blake felt herself waver.

"What?" she asked, confused.

A guttural noise tore itself out of his throat. With the sound, Ryan moved again.

Blake was ready.

She let his punch go as far as it could before grabbing onto his arm with both of her hands. Then she turned into him, her back against his chest, and used his momentum and her balance to do something her previous trainer would have been proud to see.

Ryan didn't have time to stop the flip. Blake felt his full weight for a split second while she pushed up as he went over her.

If they had been on hardwood or tile, she was sure she would have heard a loud thud. Instead all she heard was Ryan's breath being knocked out of his chest. He wheezed. Then he was coughing on the ground, staring up at the sky.

Blake wasn't through.

She took two steps over to him and grabbed his arm for the third time since they had come into the woods. It wasn't easy to do in her dress, but she managed to flip him over. He kept coughing as she pinned his arm behind his back.

She wished she had her handcuffs.

Ryan started squirming. Blake thumped the back of his head. Then she winced as something stung her eye. It took a second to realize what it was.

She cussed low.

"You busted my eyebrow, Ryan. You better have a dang good reason for—"

Footsteps were coming fast from the tree line.

Blake tightened her grip on Ryan's arm.

Someone had followed them. Had Ryan not been alone?

Suddenly Blake regretted running blindly after the man. She should have been more observant to who was around them.

Worse came to worst she could run toward the old Kmart and to the main road for help. Or hide if needed.

Or she could fight some more.

Blake was still trying to figure out her plan of fight, flight, or find a tree to hide in, when the new potential opponent entered the clearing.

She recognized him.

"Shirt Guy," she said, the first thought coming out of her mouth.

Sure enough, it was the tall good-looking man from the gym's lobby. He even still had the shirt he'd let her borrow in his hand.

It was close to the badge on his hip.

He must have been eyeing her while Blake eyed it.

"You're the sheriff," she realized.

The man was breathing hard but not out of breath. He nodded, then motioned to Ryan.

"And this is…?"

Ryan started squirming again. Blake shifted her weight to stop him.

"A victim," he yelled.

Blake snorted. She looked down at the back of his head.

"Ryan, you've never been a victim a day in your life."

"You—you don't have any right to be doing this to me," he wailed back. "Now get off before I really get mad."

Blake had no intention of doing that at all, but the sheriff cleared his throat. He had gotten closer. Blake had to crane her head up to see into his eyes.

"I might not know what's happening, but I think I can take it from here." That deep baritone sure was nice.

Still, she hesitated and glanced down at his badge.

The pain in her eyebrow disappeared. The ache in her chest that had started six months ago flared to life.

Then she relented.

THE MAN SPENT their walk back to the parking lot trying his best to damn the woman walking behind them. It wasn't until Deputy Price met them at the tree line that he shut up. And that might have had more to do with Price's reaction.

In the middle of asking what was going on, he stopped himself and openly stared at the woman.

"Blake?"

Liam turned in time to see the woman smile briefly.

"Hey there, Price. It's been a minute. How are you?"

Price's eyes were wide, his excitement showing with ease.

"What do you mean, 'how are you?' What's going on? Who is—" Price stopped himself again. Now he was focusing on the man in cuffs. Whoever he was, Price seemed to recognize him. But only after seeing the woman.

His excitement dulled.

"What are you doing here?" he asked the man.

The chatterbox suddenly didn't like talking. He didn't answer.

Liam was annoyed at the lack of context he, the sheriff, had in this situation.

He also didn't like the wandering eyes of the people still in the parking lot. He motioned to Price's cruiser.

"I want to know what's going on, but let's go to the station," he said.

"Am I under arrest?" The man broke his silence.

Liam looked over his shoulder at Blake. Blood was coming down the side of her face. Her dress was torn at its side. There was a scratch or two along her left arm. She might have had the upper hand when he had shown up, but clearly the man had gotten a few licks in. He tried to keep his anger out of his response.

"I strongly suggest we all head that way to talk."

It wasn't technically an answer, but it did the trick.

The man hushed. Price took charge of him. Then he looked to Blake.

"Do you want to ride shotgun? Or—"

Liam cut him off.

"She can ride with me. You go on ahead." Liam turned around to face her straight on. She didn't look like she was going to argue. Instead, she pulled her cell phone out.

"Let me call my ride first."

Liam gave her some space to make her call and tried his best to keep himself close enough so he was blocking her from the onlookers still meandering through the parking lot. They were lucky that most of the cars were closer to the gym.

"Okay, I'm ready," she said after a minute or so. "I guess we're heading to the sheriff's truck."

She started to walk in its direction, but Liam caught her hand.

He felt her tension like a glass of ice water to the system.

He let go immediately.

Then he pulled the shirt he had slung over his shoulder off and handed it to her.

Again.

"I think it might be for the best if you just left this on for now."

He motioned to the tear in her dress but made sure to keep his eyes on her.

She didn't need any further explanation.

"I'm not sure if this is a lucky or unlucky shirt," she said, "but thank you again."

Her smile was strained, but she put the shirt on with no complaint.

Liam nodded. They started their walk to his truck. The few bystanders left made no attempt to pretend they weren't staring.

He noticed it wasn't at him though.

All eyes followed to Blake like moths to a red-haired flame.

Once again, Liam wondered who the heck she was.

Chapter Three

The McCoy County Sheriff's Department hadn't changed much in the fifteen years since she'd last been there. Neither had the locals who still staffed its halls.

Blake followed the sheriff through the lobby, taking pains to not make eye contact with the receptionist. Mary Kimball wasn't all that bad, but Blake wasn't great at chatting with the older woman. She wasn't a gossip, but she had been known to deeply pry into anyone's personal life if given the chance.

Blake didn't want to give her that chance, so she matched the sheriff's pace until her arm brushed against his.

He glanced over her at the movement but didn't speak. He had been just as quiet in the truck before, during, and after Blake had called Lola again. She had wanted to make sure her stepmom wasn't overwhelmed with getting Clem and Bruce back home solo.

"Shondra invited us for lunch," she'd repeated. "I just changed the location to the house. She loves these babies, and me, so don't you worry. You just take care of that man Ryan. Don't worry about rushing home."

Lola was a bright rainbow of optimism and love.

The way she said "that man" was laced with disgust and anger.

It was an uncomfortable but profound change.

Blake felt it too. She knew she was going to have to share it with Sheriff Weaver.

Maybe that's why she accepted the quiet ride to the department.

She was holding on to the last vestiges of peace before Ryan took it from her.

Blake sucked in a deep breath.

By the time she exhaled, they were in one of the department meeting rooms. Price Collins was already waiting for them.

He surprised Blake with an open arm hug.

"Sheriff Trouble!" he exclaimed, encircling her in a bear hug. He wasn't a particularly large man, but the embrace was all-encompassing. Blake couldn't even return it. So she let it happen and laughed a little.

"It's been a while since I've heard that one," she said.

Price stepped back, breaking the embrace, and was all smiles.

"You make a name like that for yourself, and you better believe I'm going to use it," he said. "I've been waiting to yell it at you since I heard it. I didn't realize you were back in town yet. I guess I'm behind on town talk."

He stepped to the side and rolled a chair away from the table for her. He did the same for his boss. They were in the middle of seating themselves as Price made a more dramatic introduction.

"Sheriff Weaver, let me reintroduce you to Sheriff Blake Bennet. Also known as Sheriff Trouble by some of her colleagues at her last two departments."

Sheriff Weaver's eyebrow rose high.

Blake tried to tamp down her grimace. She wasn't a fan of having to explain her current situation in detail. This situation, however, definitely needed the context.

"I didn't cause the trouble, I just kind of followed it," she tried.

Price laughed.

"And helped fix it." He swiveled so he was facing Sheriff Weaver directly. He pointed to Blake. "This here wonder woman has been elected sheriff of *two* different departments in Georgia and Alabama. That's to say nothing of her rocketing through every law enforcement establishment she's been a part of. Her last gig made national news. She was even hailed as an integral part of helping put an end to an entire town's corruption."

Blake couldn't help but stop him there.

"I didn't realize you were keeping tabs on me, Price. I'm almost flattered." She gave him a look that she hoped showed she wasn't in the mood for being flattered. He laughed again.

"Hey, when a Seven Roads local leaves the nest as a baby bird only to go fight with lions in their dens, you take notice." He met the sheriff's eye again. "Not saying you don't do us good here, Sheriff, but I just need you to know that who you're dealing with isn't some ordinary citizen. Blake Bennet has a knack for taming trouble."

Blake was about to scold her old friend, but his demeanor changed. He softened.

She knew what came next.

"I never got to say it, but I sure was sorry about what happened. How are you doin'? How are the kids?"

If it had been a gossip or Mrs. Kimball or any other local, Blake would have been curt. Instead, she gave Price a genuine answer. It was short but it was true.

"I'm still adjusting. We all are."

Price nodded.

"If anyone can handle it, I think it's you," he said. "If you ever need anything, you can let me and my kid know. She's at the babysitting age now too and wouldn't mind it a bit."

Blake took the offer with a quick smile.

Then she looked at the sheriff.

Two thoughts immediately popped into her head.

One, Sheriff Weaver was undeniably good-looking. Whether it was in a gym lobby, a parking lot, between the trees, or in a room full of fluorescents, the man was captivatingly handsome.

Two, despite his good looks and status as Seven Roads's main protector, he had no idea who she was.

Or, more accurately, what Price was talking about.

He didn't seem confused, but there was definitely a look of trying to connect the pieces he had just been given.

Blake felt the warmth of his shirt around her and decided to give him a hand.

"I moved back to Seven Roads a few months ago to take care of my niece and nephew," she said, trying to keep her voice as steady as possible. "My sister passed away six months ago, and now I'm their legal guardian. My niece was the one today who talked about moths and butterflies at the daycare assembly."

Blake gave another little smile. She hoped to undercut the potential pity coming her way. Thankfully, the sheriff didn't give it. At least he didn't give too much.

"I'm sorry for your loss." Then a slight pivot that she appreciated. "And I remember your niece. She spoke well."

Blake felt some pride at that. She merely accepted the compliment with a nod though. Then it was down to business.

"How does Ryan Reed figure into everything?" he asked. "You two clearly know him, but I've never run into him since I took up my badge."

Blake wasn't surprised. In fact, the only surprise she had was that Ryan had shown up in Seven Roads at all. She had been sure he wouldn't dare after their last encounter.

"Ryan was my sister Beth's brother-in-law," she explained.

"Former brother-in-law. Beth and his brother, Tim, divorced right after my nephew was born."

Blake cut her gaze to Price. She tried to find tactful words.

"Tim wasn't the best of guys," she continued. "He gave up his rights to the kids after letting anyone who would listen know that he didn't want to lose his life by being a father. After the divorce was finalized, he left town and moved somewhere up north. As far as I know, no one's heard from him since. He didn't even show up for Beth's funeral."

Old but violent rage welled up inside of Blake. She slipped her hand onto her lap and balled it into a fist. Her nails bit into the skin of her palm. Both men showed their displeasure. Price was shaking his head. The sheriff's frown was deep.

"Ryan, however, did," she kept on. "He pulled me aside and started asking about money. He kept wondering what I'd do now that I was back in town. If I'd get into the sheriff's department or if I'd sit around using up Beth's life insurance money to keep the kids and me going." Tiny points of pain radiated into her palm as Blake applied more pressure. "He didn't once ask about how the kids were doing otherwise."

"He was also really loud about the rest, from what I heard," Price added.

Blake nodded. She'd had no doubt that word would travel fast after Ryan had been so loud at the funeral. She had been relieved, however, to hear that the rumor mill hadn't churned out every detail. Maybe that had been more to Lola's credit than anything. Blake had long suspected that her stepmother had worked overtime to try to keep as much idle chatter about their family's tragedy under wraps as possible over the last six months or so. It was no one's business but their own that Blake was currently using her own life savings to take time off from working and make their transition as easy as possible. The insurance money was currently in a savings account that she wasn't touching unless absolutely necessary.

She hadn't told Ryan any of that.

And she definitely wouldn't.

"So this is the first time you've seen Ryan since the funeral?" the sheriff asked.

Blake nodded again.

"He doesn't, and hasn't, lived in Seven Roads for years, as far as I know," she said. "So seeing him at the school caught me off guard. I was going to go ask why he was there, but he started running. Past job experiences had me run after him on instinct."

"Did he say anything to you?" he asked.

"He asked where 'it' was and said he knows that I'm working on it. I have no idea what he's talking about." A cruel thought ran across her mind. "Unless he's referring to the insurance money Beth left behind."

Maybe it was her imagination, but Blake could have sworn she saw the sheriff's jaw twitch. Sheriff Weaver pushed his chair back with a little force too.

"Only one way to find out," he said. "I'll be right back."

Blake did the small-talk dance with Price while the sheriff interviewed Ryan. She caught up on his daughter's life, some mutual friends from school chatter, and then lightly on some of the bigger changes in town. That small talk had no choice but to lead back to the Grayton Steel Mill accident. It had been one of the most sensational things to happen in Seven Roads in the last few years.

"You know Mr. Grant's son started working a lot harder after the accident," Price made a point to say. "His name's Elijah. I met him once. He isn't as much of a social butterfly as his dad. He doesn't seem to need the attention. Still, I heard he stays at the mill enough that he's won over some of the workers. There was even some talk that they want him to take over the place instead of his daddy."

Blake didn't know how to feel about the steel mill anymore. Growing up, it had always just been a place that employed half the town. Even after the accident, it still was just the steel mill.

But then, one day, it became the last place that Beth had been seen alive.

She had finished her safety inspection and then gotten into the car accident on the way home.

It hadn't been the steel mill's fault, but now Blake felt an uncomfortable weight at its mention.

Still, she found the news interesting.

"I figured after Mr. Clearwater retired and shut down the tractor supply biz, his bestie Mr. Grant would eventually follow his lead," she admitted. "He's probably prepping his kid to take over for him. I doubt he'd just shut the mill down instead. The entire town would revolt."

Price agreed with that. Like her, he had grown up with the steel mill being the heart of the town's workforce. The idea of it shutting down was as bizarre as if Corrie Daniels decided to keep gossip to herself.

Not long after, the sheriff finally reappeared. He wasn't happy. Neither was Blake once she heard Ryan's excuse for his sudden reappearance.

Men lied, women too, but Ryan Reed was the worst of those who chose to twist the truth. He had been the same way before the divorce and shortly after. Lola had been livid recounting the way he had been loudly saying the entire thing was Beth's fault and none of it was his brother's fault. That's why Blake had a hard time believing anything the sheriff was saying. Then again, Weaver looked like he wasn't exactly buying it either.

"Ryan said he was in the area, saw the daycare program,

and was curious," the sheriff continued to relay. "He claims he wasn't going to try to talk to you or the kids at all. He just wanted a peek at them to see how they were doing. He was trying to be inconspicuous, best I can guess."

Blake crossed her arms over her chest and snorted.

"When I saw him, he sure wasn't trying to seem inconspicuous. If he was Waldo, then every reader looking for him would have been disappointed at how easy it was to spot him."

Sheriff Weaver, leaning against the table, also had his arms crossed over his chest. Blake thought she saw his lips twitch. She continued with the other part of Ryan's sudden reappearance that had her questioning the man.

"Also, why the heck did he run?"

At this, the sheriff did a finger gun at her.

"I asked that actually," he said. He cleared his throat and surprised Blake with a mock impression of Ryan. It was a nasally sound that must have been hard for his naturally deep voice. "'I ran because she chased me like a bat outta hell.'"

Blake rolled her eyes.

"I took one step toward him, and he was the one out there running a relay." Blake leaned forward. "Not to mention, once I finally got him to stop, he attacked like a feral animal being caged. Why would you do that if you were only there with the best of intentions?"

The sheriff's gaze went to the Band-Aid over her eyebrow. It wasn't the best patch job she had done on herself, but it would do until she could take more care at the house.

"Has he never been physical before?" he asked.

Blake shook her head.

"Ryan, and Tim for that matter, have always been slimy guys but never abusive."

The sheriff tilted his head now a little.

"What about you?" he asked. "Have you gotten physical with him before?"

Blake snorted.

"I've wanted to smack both brothers upside the head since Tim married into the family." She sighed out long. "But I didn't want to upset my sister. Or my dad. So I only told my piece once about not liking them. I never brought it up again, especially after Clem was born."

Another, different kind of resentment pooled inside of Blake. She didn't often talk about her father, not even with her stepmother. He didn't live with them and, as far as Blake could guess, never would. Blake had only ever fallen short in her father's eyes. Nothing had changed that, even after Beth's passing.

Not even his optimistic and loving wife could sway Blake's father to change his poor opinion of her.

That was one reason Lola had moved in—she couldn't stand to see no one helping. So she had stepped in without a word.

Blake shifted in her seat, uncomfortable.

She shook her head.

"I've given Ryan no reason to run from me or attack me like that," she underlined. "And other than a hospital visit after Bruce was born, as far as I know, neither Ryan nor Tim have shown any interest in either him or Clementine."

The sheriff pushed off the table. His arms stayed crossed.

It sure was a powerful stance. Blake could imagine his campaign to be sheriff must have had some good-looking ad and marketing materials.

Price was silent but was obviously not a fan of the story either.

"It's up to you if you want to press charges, but just know he's already talked about reaching out to a lawyer," the sheriff said. "Plus, you did chase him into the woods. Even if you were only following him to talk."

Blake already knew she looked like the instigator in the situation. Still, it made her snarl.

The sheriff didn't directly address the less-than-professional noise. Then again, it wasn't like she was at work here. She was just a citizen now.

"I'll leave then," she said, standing. "I assume talking to him beforehand would be discouraged."

"Strongly so," Weaver agreed. "Unless you want to keep dealing with him and his lawyer too."

Blake didn't want that. Plus, she needed to get home. Lola was already a saint for sacrificing her retirement to help Blake and the kids. She didn't need to add a new stressor to their already chaotic lives.

"I think this morning was enough of a detour for us."

The sheriff nodded.

"Good choice."

A moment of silence bubbled up between them. Sheriff Weaver wasn't the least talkative man she had met, but with his size and demeanor, that quiet had its own presence. One that made her feel a bit squirmy.

"Can I go now, or do I need to do anything else?" she asked, trying to move away from yet another uncomfortable feeling.

He nodded to Price.

"Price can drop you off at your house whenever you're ready. We'll let Mr. Reed go after you've already left." He took something from his pocket and handed it over.

It was his business card.

Liam Weaver, Sheriff

"You can call the department or me directly if there's any more trouble with him. It would be faster to call the department though."

Blake nodded. She didn't have her purse or a pocket to put it in, so she held it against the side of her dress. She suddenly felt a wave of vulnerability in wearing it. Or, really, wearing it without some kind of badge out in front.

Her eyes flitted to the sheriff's star. She averted her gaze right after.

"Hopefully I won't have to use it," she said. "But thanks."

The sheriff didn't hesitate.

"Hopefully not." He walked to the door and opened it wide. A deputy was walking by. The sheriff caught his attention. "Make sure Mr. Reed doesn't leave until Miss Bennet here is gone. I don't want him starting anything in the parking lot."

Blake spied the deputy's name tag: Mel Gavin.

He looked familiar, but the name wasn't landing.

That was okay though. She had no intention of making friends at the moment. Even reconnecting with Price wasn't going to go past their shared ride.

It couldn't.

Blake had enough to deal with. Enough to juggle. Enough to worry about.

She smiled up at the sheriff, thanked him again, and started to walk on by.

His eyes followed her every step of the way.

Maybe if things had been different, Blake would have said something more. Done something more.

Instead, she let the smile be the end of it.

It wasn't until she was sitting the car with Price later that she realized she was still wearing the sheriff's shirt.

Chapter Four

The sunset was nice. Liam watched it from his apartment's balcony with a beer in one hand and his phone in the other.

A call he was waiting for hadn't come. He figured it wouldn't.

Still, he had waited.

It wasn't until the sun had completely gone that he put the phone down on the balcony's table.

A few minutes later, a rock hit the chair arm next to it. Liam set down his beer as another small rock came over the balcony railing at him.

"You know, throwing rocks at the sheriff isn't the smartest move," he called out.

Laughter came back.

"Is your door unlocked?" the voice from the ground asked.

"No."

A groan sounded.

Liam stood.

"You have thirty seconds," he called out again.

The sound of footsteps running to the outdoor stairwell echoed behind him as Liam made his way back into the apartment. He didn't slow his steps even a little. Yet when he unlocked the front door, a second later it was opening. Theo Chasten was out of breath but grinning.

"I'm—I'm getting faster," he panted. "I even skipped like six steps coming—coming up here."

Liam backtracked to the kitchen. He pointed to the refrigerator as he set his aim to the balcony again.

"There's leftovers in the fridge, superstar."

He didn't have to say any more than that. Which was a relief. Liam had come to Seven Roads after a divorce had left him tapped out on being any kind of social. He'd wanted quiet; he'd wanted peace.

Then he'd run into a teenaged boy sitting in the stairwell of their apartment complex while a storm raged on a few feet outside. Theo had been quiet then, but a strong quiet. It wasn't fear or worry that kept his mouth shut tight. It was his choice. His armor. Getting him to admit he was locked out of his apartment and unable to get a hold of his mother had been a chore. If it hadn't been for the tornado sirens going off, Liam doubted he could have convinced the teen to seek shelter in his apartment until his mom came home.

But those sirens went off and Theo had begrudgingly taken Liam up on the offer.

It was the first time Theo had been given help without asking for it but not the last. Now, almost two years later, Liam had become a mentor of sorts to the boy. He helped him with school, made sure he ate well, and answered any life questions that came his way. Liam had even taught the boy how to drive. Though, no one had been happy during that ordeal.

Liam had been deployed in combat zones before. Teaching an anxious teen to drive had tested his nerves almost as much.

In the end, it all led to Theo finally not fighting the offer of food anymore. It saved them both more time and Liam more sanity.

"Also grab you a water, fast guy," he added. "Because I

can almost bet you haven't had a drop all day. Just that energy drink crap or sodas."

Theo laughed from the kitchen.

"You sure do know me really well, Sheriff." He cleared his throat. When he spoke again, his accent had more syrup in it. "Much obliged."

The night air was cool but not cold enough that the balcony door could stay open without messing with the air conditioner. Without saying it, though, Theo slid the glass door closed when he came out. It was little things like that that made Liam realize how much his relationship with the sixteen-year-old had changed since they had met.

First there had been yelling.

Then there had been annoyance.

Now Theo threw rocks, Liam left him food, and the former thought about the AC.

"Didn't you have a study group tonight? Don't tell me you bailed to come hang out with me. You'll never get that girl's attention if you aren't actually there to get it."

Theo dropped down into his usual spot on the chair next to Liam. He was already in the process of eating the leftovers.

"Her name is Sammy, thank you very much," he said around some food in his mouth. "And she's the reason I bailed. She had to babysit her little sister so her parents could go somewhere."

"Is the rest of the study group still meeting up?"

Liam saw the boy's head nod forward in the near darkness.

"Yeah but I'm not about to go sit in some coffee shop with a bunch of people I don't even talk to only to pretend that I'm not good at calculus."

Liam held in a chuckle at that.

Theo Chasten was a smart aleck, but there was a heavy emphasis on the smart part. Liam had been quick to pick up on the fact that Theo's mom wasn't exactly one to dote on her son. She worked hard, it was true, but she often overlooked him and his needs. He'd already been dropped into foster care once as a younger kid. He didn't talk about that time much though. Once his mom worked her plan to get him back, she'd done enough to keep him out. Still, that had weighed heavy on his little shoulders, and he had acted out more than not when he was younger. It had earned him a less-than-favorable reputation in town.

Most of Seven Roads had written him off already, thinking he didn't know a thing. Liam, his teachers, and thankfully Theo himself knew otherwise. Though that didn't mean he wanted others to know it. He hid his capabilities behind a facade of teenage angst and annoyance, especially from his peers.

"Plus," Theo continued, "I heard you chased some woman through the woods today, so I thought I'd rather waste my time here talking to you."

The image of Blake Bennet perfectly popped up in Liam's mind. Standing there in a ripped yellow dress wearing his shirt, which swallowed her, her eyebrows scrunched, the Band-Aid she had applied moving as she was thoughtful. Sending her off with Deputy Price had bothered him more than it should have.

"I didn't chase a woman through the woods. I chased after a man *she* was chasing," he corrected. Liam took a pull from his beer. "But that whole thing hasn't been resolved, so I'm not talking about it here."

The shadow of Theo's head bobbed again.

"I figured you weren't out there terrorizing civilians today," he said. "Especially not when I heard it was that sheriff lady. What do you call a former sheriff, by the way? Is it like the president, where you still call them Sheriff even though they've left the office? Or is it more like *Star Trek* and once you've left the captain's chair you're just whatever position you're in?"

Liam quickly sidestepped the additional ramble and instead got to the part that surprised him.

"You know Blake Bennet?"

His question came out a little strong. Luckily, Theo didn't pick up on it.

"I know *of* her, but I've only seen her once or twice in person," he answered. "Some of the workers at the steel mill have talked about her. Apparently, she was on TV a few times. It sounded like she upset a lot of people where she used to live."

Liam started to fiddle with the label on his bottle.

"People at the factory were talking about her?" This wasn't the first time that Theo, working part-time in the cafeteria, had gotten him an inside scoop.

"You've heard about her too. Or at least her sister. You know that guy, Hector Martinez, the guy Missy Clearwater was really good friends with before her own life got depressing, who got really badly burned when one of the furnaces started melting down a while back? That sheriff lady's sister was the safety person who came out to do a safety report on it. Later she got into a car accident on the county road. You know, the gnarly one that had every ambulance in the county there."

The label on the bottle started to slide off. Liam paused. Then it finally clicked.

"Beth Bennet." He swore under his breath. "I knew the name sounded familiar."

Liam remembered the accident that had killed Blake's sister. He hadn't been in town for it, but the briefing had been enough when he'd come back. Doc Ernest had been visibly upset. The only solace she had given was that the woman had been killed instantly in the rollover. Her funeral had been a private event. Liam had meant to send his condolences but hadn't been able to find the right time.

Then, he felt ashamed to think, he had forgotten. His mind had gone to cases and work, and now here he was putting together old pieces to a current puzzle.

"Apparently she's been in town for a while now, but no one's really seen her," Theo went on. "The talk from the cafeteria wasn't exactly nice about her either. They talked about her trying really hard to stay out of sight, but it also sounded like they didn't try to go see her at all either."

There was distaste in the teen's words. For good reason, he'd never been a fan of public opinion.

Liam went back to slowly peeling off the label of his bottle. He tried to keep his tone casual.

"Is there anything else you heard about her? The sheriff, I mean." Liam regretted how *not* casual-sounding the question came out.

He had overreached. Judging by the quick head turn, Theo had realized it too.

"Whoa, whoa, whoa!" he exclaimed. "Did I hear that right? Is our dear sheriff finally, *finally* giving in to the drama that is Seven Roads and its people? Are you really sitting here trying to gossip with me?"

Liam rolled his eyes and made sure the breath he let out was unmistakably annoyed.

"All right," he said. "I think this conversation has run its course."

He started to get up, but Theo grabbed at the leg of his jeans. He was laughing.

"Calm down there, Sheriff," he said. "No need to get all defensive. Everyone in town knows you don't put up with the rumor mill. I was just thrown a little, is all."

Liam stayed where he was.

He knew he had successfully moved the boy out of his teasing and right to where he wanted him—answering his original question without additional commentary.

"The only other thing I know about the Bennet family is that they used to be one of the longtime families of Seven Roads, but then everyone started leaving. The lady who passed was the last one who was here before her sister showed up again. Seems like there was family drama before that." He shut the leftover container with a click. His next words sounded thoughtful. "If the sheriff has been back for a while, then she really must have tried hard to keep to herself. I mean, it's hard not to notice someone in this place after all."

He wasn't wrong. Seven Roads was thimble-sized small. Even if you wanted to stay off the radar, a local would put you right back on it the second you stepped foot into any store or venue. Maybe that was some of the hesitance he'd seen in Blake before the daycare program. It was the general public that had her wavering outside of the gym doors.

If that was true, then it also made Liam even more irritated with Ryan Reed.

It sounded like Blake had earned her right to silence, and he'd gone and forced her into the public eye.

Theo quieted after that. Liam too. Eventually the teen pulled out his homework. He went to bed as soon as it was finished.

His mother had never once been against Liam stepping in to help take care of Theo. The guest bedroom was more his room than the teen's own bedroom in the apartment on the first floor. Still, there were moments when Liam wished the boy wouldn't come by. That he would, instead, find comfort and happiness in his own home.

But life didn't always work out as easy as that.

Theo knew that. Liam knew that.

Blake Bennet knew that too.

Liam's hip ached a little. He kneaded it with his fist and then checked his phone one last time for the night.

There was no reason for her to call or text.

Still, he checked.

There was nothing and he decided that was that.

Today had been an offshoot of his investigation. A side quest that had concluded, and now he had to get back to the main one.

Missy Clearwater.

The young woman whose last two weeks of existence had been sad enough for everyone to believe that her taking her own life made more sense than someone else being responsible. Though Doc Ernest was sure to give credit to the ones that had, in most people's opinion, been the motivation behind her action.

"Blunt trauma killed her," Doc Ernest had announced once she had reconsidered her autopsy conclusions. "But if you ask me, it's the ones closest to her that got her falling off that bridge. She has a big fight with her dad that everyone hears about, then her boyfriend leaves her, only to get with her best friend a week later?" Doc Ernest had shaken her head, sorrow lining her features. "That's a rough go of it, especially on someone so young and sweet as Missy."

But Liam couldn't ignore the suspicion that the flash drive had created. It had spider-webbed through every story he heard, through the autopsy report, through the town chatter, and through the evidence they did have.

That's why he wasn't going to stop until he could put those suspicions to rest. Or find out what had really happened.

Which is why he needed to talk to Cassandra about Missy's last interaction.

It could either help him move on or give him something to go on to find another piece to the puzzle.

Blake Bennet might have been intriguing, but her time with him was obviously done. She had her own life to live while he had Missy's death to put to rest.

Yet, when the next morning rolled around, Liam found the woman leaning against his truck in the parking lot of the gas station. It was all he could do to hide his surprise.

"I've thought about it," Blake said in greeting with all the confidence in the world, "and I'm pretty sure I can help you. And I think you should let me."

Chapter Five

"You think you can help me."

The sheriff's baritone sure was something, even repeating her own words right back to her. Blake pushed off the truck and nodded, resolute. She held up the second reason she had come to find the man before explaining.

"There's also this," she said. "Your shirt washed, dried, and ironed with care. You wouldn't even know it's been through the wringer."

The button-up had gone directly into the washer when Blake had gotten home from the sheriff's department. She had never been the best at remembering the laundry in a timely manner, but when it came to this particular denim shirt, she had been unusually attentive. It had, after all, helped cover her as much as its owner had. It only seemed right to be just as courteous.

The sheriff eyed the shirt with a raised brow. She thought he was going to refuse the gesture for a second, but then he grabbed it and held it against his side with the one arm and kept his coffee in his other. The man was a Ralph Lauren ad come to life as far as Blake was concerned.

"You didn't have to do all that," he said, tipping his chin a little to get a better angle on her gaze. "But thanks."

Blake waved the comment off.

"I might have been a little chaotic recently, but I'm not without manners. Plus, if I hadn't done it, Lola wouldn't have let me hear the end of it. Lola being my mom. Aka the lady who will have my hide if I don't have all my social p's and q's together."

Sheriff Weaver snorted.

Blake paused in what she had intended to say next.

The sheriff looked right near caught.

His humored expression smoothed.

She wasn't letting him go.

"What was that for?" she asked.

He didn't hesitate.

"What was what for?"

Blake crossed her arms over her chest. She gave him a mock snort, then pointed to herself.

"You snorted at me just now. I want to know why." She tilted her head to the side and feigned politeness. "Don't tell me you've got something against people washing your clothes at home. What was I supposed to do? Dry-clean it?" Blake glanced down at the shirt that was pinned against him. "No offense, but it's not *that* nice of a shirt."

This time there was no snort, but she could have sworn a smile was trying to tug up at the edges of his lips. It failed.

"You said you washed my shirt because of good manners. Then you said you only did it because of your mother. You only were nice because of the consequence of not being so. I just think it's funny how you contradicted yourself so fast."

Blake opened her mouth.

Then she shut it.

Her face was growing hot. Her words would come out boiling next if she didn't calm down.

So she decided to acknowledge instead of defend herself.

"Hey, not all of us can be so domestic," she said. "Just because I had a consequence that forced my hand doesn't mean I also didn't have good intentions. It's like baking a cake for someone's birthday. Normally most people don't bake cakes at random for you, but if they miss giving you one on your birthday that's kind of a bummer. I did it because those are the unwritten rules, but I also genuinely wanted to be helpful after everything that happened. So follow the same rules and say thank you and let's move on."

The sheriff wasn't smiling. He wasn't frowning either.

Blake took that as acceptance. His nod helped prove it further.

"I suppose you're right about that. Thank you."

Blake felt like she had given the man some humble pie.

No sooner had she felt some satisfaction did she have to eat a slice herself.

The sheriff had the audacity to start walking around her toward his truck door.

"That's it?" she asked, doing a little hop, skip, and shuffle to follow. "I didn't tell you what I could help you with yet."

She stopped between him and the driver's-side door, sliding in before he could even reach the handle. His eyebrow rose again at the move. Blake watched it with a surge of annoyance. His tone when he spoke next didn't help.

"I didn't ask for anything from you. So don't worry yourself over me."

His eyes dropped to the door handle next to her.

She took a deep breath and moved out of the way. She could fight him, get huffier and turn into a Southern woman who just so happened to be a former sheriff, but instead, Blake decided to play it as cool as she could. She had dealt with strong-willed people all her life. Just because this one was a sheriff didn't mean a thing.

She watched him open his door, deposit the shirt on the

passenger's seat, and place his coffee in the cup holder, all like he didn't have an audience.

When he settled into his seat and went to close the door, Blake cleared her throat and threw bait in the water.

"I can give you Cassandra West."

Blake was ready to add context, but something changed. The man's entire body tensed. His brows went up. His eyes found and then swallowed hers. She didn't need to give him anything more.

He was already hooked.

"What do you mean, you can 'give me Cassandra West'?" he asked.

Blake took a small step forward and lowered her voice.

"When Price was driving me home yesterday, he mentioned you had been having a hard time getting her to talk to you. Since she seems to be skirting you, I'm assuming it's not for a case. At least not one where your badge would work, or else you would have already had her talking." Blake patted her chest. "I can get you a casual conversation with her."

"*You're* friends with Cassandra West?"

Blake didn't like his tone. Hers came out a little huffier, regardless of trying to remain completely civil.

"We go way back. She'll talk if I'm there. Of that, I'm sure."

"If you're there," he deadpanned.

"If I'm there," she repeated.

Blake took another small step forward. She made a show of turning her wrist over to look at her watch.

"And, as it so happens, my presence can be helpful right about now." Blake gave the man a big old grin. "What do you say, Sheriff? Do you want my help or not?"

A part of Blake expected the man to grumble or try to

dissuade the notion that he needed help. Instead, he surprised her.

He nodded.

"Your car or mine?"

Blake mentally hiccupped. Her face started to heat.

Both states made her mentally scold herself.

"Follow me in yours, or else the whole town will be talking about us riding together," she said, regaining her composure. "Meeting up is fine, showing up together will get everyone's mouths flapping."

He nodded again.

"After you," he said, motioning out to the parking lot.

And that was that.

Blake had hooked the sheriff and would be repaying her debt to him. All while the kids were in daycare and Lola was out being social.

It felt good.

It felt—

"Miss Bennet?"

Blake's body turned back on reflex.

"Yeah?"

The sheriff wasn't smiling, but she heard something different in his tone when he spoke.

"Call me Liam."

THERE WERE TWO cars parked outside of the Twenty-Two Coffee Shop. Liam let Blake take the last open parking spot, and he slid his truck into the drug store's lot across the street. By the time he was crossing over Main on foot, Blake was standing on the sidewalk and staring up at the café's sign. Her hair was loose. It looked nice against the light-colored blouse she was wearing. Her expression, however, was flitting between a scowl and a smirk.

When she saw him, she nodded up to the sign.

"We might have all gotten older, but some things really haven't changed a bit."

Liam waited for an explanation. Blake didn't give one.

"Make sure you order something frilly-sounding," she followed up instead. "You don't want to offend Corrie."

"Why? She doesn't own this place."

Blake snorted.

"No, but Cassandra does, and if you make Corrie happy, Cassandra will follow. Same with the opposite end of the experience. Make one twin angry, you get the other one angry too." That scowl-smirk combo smoothed into an easy-to-define feeling. She gave him a raised brow. "Don't tell me you've been in Seven Roads for two years, and this is the first you're hearing of the twins. The Daniels family is a part of town lore 101."

Blake didn't give him space to respond.

He was finding she was a point-A-to-point-B kind of woman. She didn't stray from her target. At least, not long enough for him to get a few more words in.

Liam wasn't sure if he disliked that quality though. The South had a habit of churning out people who spent more time talking about nothing than not. At least with Blake, she seemed to edit out the time-wasting part.

The little bell over the front door dinged as she led the way inside of the shop. Liam had been in the café several times but had never really lingered. It was a small space with only a handful of tables and chairs and a bar that took up more than half of the tight area. Having a quiet cup of coffee to himself had never been an option in the shop. Their to-go service had been his best plan.

Now he settled into a chair next to one of the larger plate glass windows that looked out at the sidewalk that wrapped around the edge of the corner lot. The old pocked road that led from Main to one of the older established neighborhoods was in desperate need of repair. According to Mayor Tufton, that was an almost impossible task given their current town funds.

Mayor Tufton and his little sports car never drove down Main unless it was campaign time.

The mayor had a habit of keeping his head down outside of town repair too. The moment he had heard that Liam was still looking into Missy's death had been the moment he had decided to have a lot of opinions on why they *shouldn't* have a lot of opinions on the matter.

It was true that Liam had no solid evidence to suggest that anything had happened to Missy other than her jumping off the bridge, but it still made Liam angry now at how the mayor's reasoning for stopping had been about "the optics." The mayor didn't want bad press.

Liam curled his fist against the knee of his jeans.

Blake didn't notice. Instead, her attention seemed to have gone behind them and out of the room.

She didn't sigh, but when she spoke, her words were heavy.

"If Corrie's here, she'll come out first, and she'll talk our ears off, but I'm hoping that since all I saw was Cassandra's car, we're safe for now. If not, we'll just have to endure."

Liam tilted his head to the side in question.

"You haven't lived in Seven Roads in years, how are you so sure they'll even mind you're here?"

He didn't mean it to sound as patronizing as it did, but Liam also couldn't deny he was genuinely curious. Even Theo had talked about this Bennet woman with reverence. He didn't understand why Blake was so interesting to the whole town. Was it because she had been a sheriff outside? One who had made the news?

Was it because her sister had been killed?

Sure, that warranted talk, Liam understood that, but where was this confidence stemming from? Why did Blake Bennet know she would be treated so differently?

Was it because she was beautiful?

The thought crossed Liam's mind as the woman smiled. Her hair was lit up by the sun pouring through the window. Its red seemed to liven into something warmer than before she had sat down.

Her words were still on the cold side.

"Because a long time ago, a teenager promised she would never come back in a very public way." A door opened behind the bar. Liam kept his eyes on Blake as she finished. "That teenager was wrong. Now I'm back and the townspeople want me to eat crow for it."

Her eyes attached to the woman who took a pointed path toward them.

Liam recognized her as none other than Corrie Daniels.

"Well, if it isn't Blake Bennet here in front of me again!"

Corrie stopped beside their table with a thin smile. Liam had interacted with her enough to not be a novelty, but his relationship with her was, at best, a passing acquaintance.

Then again, he could have been her flesh and blood, and she probably wouldn't have cared. Like Blake had predicted, the woman's focus attached to Blake and didn't let go. She had her hands clasped in front of her, and that smile went from thin to overbearing in a flash.

A shark in the waters who smelled blood.

"What can I say, running into you yesterday helped open my eyes to the fact that I needed to get out and be more social," Blake returned. Her words were as genuine as Corrie's smile. She motioned to the bar. "I mean, I didn't even realize that you and Cassandra took over the old coffee place and turned it into your dream shop. You've been wanting to open Twenty-Two since we were, what, sixteen? I can't believe it's taken me this long to finally visit."

Corrie couldn't have smiled any wider. Yet Liam felt like she was stretching herself. She laughed lightly.

"I can't believe you even remember something like that," Corrie said. "It was so long ago. I figured you had probably forgotten all about us since you left. To be honest, there were a few times between then and now that I'd forgotten all about that girl who fought her daddy in the park. Now I'm hearing that you had to come back and fight with someone else too."

Liam didn't understand the first reference, but he knew Corrie meant Ryan in the second. He also knew that Blake had been absolutely right. Corrie was trying to hit a nerve.

And, he might not be familiar with entire account of Blake Bennet's backstory, but he could see that a nerve had definitely been struck.

Blake's expression pulled tight. Her shoulders lined with undeniable tension.

That wasn't going to do.

Liam cleared his throat and put his cellphone on the table with a thud.

Corrie didn't seem too keen on redirecting her attention, but she did so with that customer service polite on.

"Sorry to interrupt you two playing catch-up," Liam started, "but I've been told that the faster I try your newest coffee, the faster I'll be happy. And, well, I'm sure not going to turn down happy today. Could I trouble you for the newest coffee item on the menu?"

Liam watched as her eyes widened a little. Probably because it was the most he had ever said to her. Or, maybe, Corrie was finally realizing who exactly had come in with Blake. She glanced between them but nodded.

"As it would happen, our new frozen mocha has been all the rage recently," she responded. "I would be more than happy to get you one, Sheriff."

"I'd like just a black coffee, if you don't mind," Blake added. "No whip."

Corrie did seem to mind, but she nodded all the same.

"Sure thing. I'll be back in a jiffy."

Liam waited until he was sure she was out of earshot. He fixed Blake with a narrow-eyed look.

"I thought you said to order something fancy-sounding or we'd offend them," he pointed out.

This time, Blake did sigh.

"I wanted you to order something fancy so *you* wouldn't offend them." Her gaze fell to her hand. She was rubbing her thumb along her index finger. It was like her focus shifted with it to something else entirely. Still, she finished explaining. "Me simply being back in Seven Roads has already offended them enough. There's nothing I can do to fix that. Now, if you'll excuse me, I need to use the restroom."

It happened then, as he watched her walk away.

Liam realized that his singular mission to solve the circumstances behind Missy's death had picked up another mission along the way.

Finding out who exactly Blake Bennet was.

Chapter Six

"I lied to the sheriff for you."

Blake was sitting on the edge of the back office's desk and trying to find a candy from the candy dish that she wanted to eat. Cassandra West was watching the attempt from her office chair, no doubt frowning.

"That's a bad habit to start," Cassandra replied. "I'd think someone like you, who held the same title in the past, would avoid such mistakes."

Blake grinned. She found a golden-wrapped toffee and went to work peeling back the paper.

"I lied saying I was going to the bathroom for your benefit, not mine," she said. "So save your judgment for the end of his program, thank you very much."

Cassandra let out a breath that wobbled. She was stressed. That didn't stop her from trying to cover up that fact.

"I didn't ask you for anything. Especially lying."

Blake waved the comment off with her hand and popped the candy in her mouth. It tasted like visiting her grandmother's. She rolled her neck around and met Cassandra's eye.

"No, but I figured I'd buy you some time to tell me why you're avoiding the sheriff out there," she said. "I heard he's been trying to talk to you, and you've been doing anything but."

Cassandra was the same age as Blake, which made her twin, Corrie, the same age as well. Yet Cassandra had always seemed older. Maternal, a worrier. She was also practical and leaned more conservative, especially in comparison to her sister. If Blake had to guess, she was the one who kept the coffee shop running, the workers paid, and she dealt with the day-to-day stresses of owning a business.

Cassandra was a straight shooter.

Which was why Blake didn't understand her hesitance with Liam.

"I'm not avoiding the sheriff," Cassandra defended. "I'm just not seeking him, or any sheriffs, out. It's not like I'm under investigation. I don't have to chat with him."

Blake sucked on her hard candy for a few beats. Cassandra's gaze didn't waver.

She apparently had grown up into a straight, stubborn shooter.

"Listen, I'm only here because the sheriff helped me out," Blake started. "And he seems to be really in need of talking to you. You don't have to say anything to him, but at least tell me what's going on, and let's see if I can't get him off your back." Cassandra didn't look too sure. Blake flashed her a smile. "You know me, Cassie. The good, the bad, the ugly. Whatever your personal feelings are for me, you have to know I'm not here to cause trouble. I've had enough of that for a lifetime. Now tell me why Sheriff Weaver thinks you're the answer to whatever question he has."

Blake's smile dissolved.

Cassandra looked like she had aged ten years within the last minute. She shook her head but spoke all the same. Blake put her hand back in the candy dish and twirled the candies around while the other woman explained.

"Missy Clearwater," she said, defeat in each syllable. "The

reason for her death is what he's after. Did you manage to hear about it? Or has your seclusion only let in food delivery and Walmart runs?"

Blake sidestepped the barb and recalled that the news had indeed reached her through Lola's social circle. The news had been sad, but she'd been dealing with a lot at the time. She hadn't thought too much about it past a wave of sympathy. She might have known most of the Seven Roads locals, but she'd never met the young Missy.

"I heard about her passing. Her daddy is Jonathan Clearwater, the owner of the tractor supply before he retired and sold, right?"

"Yeah, that's him." A grimace passed over Cassandra's face. "He was a big part of her problems. After he shut the tractor supply down and laid everyone off, a lot of people were angry. It's not like we have a big job pool here, you know? Especially the older folks who'd been there for a minute. But it's not exactly like they could have told him off or said anything but nice words in his direction. So they turned to the safer option of pushing that frustration onto the easier target. People were passive-aggressive and sometimes outright rude to Missy. Nothing too bad in the beginning, but after a while, it became a thing that had people whispering whenever she was around. She must've gone to her dad about it, but it backfired. They had a big fight near the diner. Yelling so loud that Mrs. Thomas almost made them leave."

Cassandra cast her a look. If she had been Corrie, she would have no doubt commented on the similarities of the last part with Blake's own past, but thankfully, she stayed on topic. She leaned back slightly, shaking her head a little more.

"Then her boyfriend went and left her—Corrie thinks because he couldn't take the unflattering spotlight—and *then* to make matters worse, he had the gall to start dating her best friend. Like it was out of a sitcom or something. They're still together, by the way. I sold them coffee last week."

Blake didn't have any other words than "Yeesh."

Cassandra seconded the sentiment.

"If that wasn't enough of a sad story, Missy died a week after that news broke. She was found beneath the bridge out at Becker Farm."

Blake stopped twirling her hand through the candy dish. That part she hadn't heard through Lola's rumor mill.

"Did she fall or jump?"

Hesitation. It lined every beat of time between Blake's question and Cassandra's answer. When it broke, her words had become notably colder.

"She was found at the bottom, in the dirt. That's all I know."

Blake averted her eyes to the dish.

"What did the newspaper say?"

There was no hesitation this time.

"That Missy jumped."

"And what does the sheriff out there think?"

No hesitation again.

"From what I've heard, that she didn't."

"He thinks she fell?" Blake asked the question, but she suspected that wasn't the answer.

"You'd have to ask him that."

Cassandra sighed out long and loud. Her patience with Blake seemed to be running out. So Blake went in for one last go.

"Why is he barking around your tree then?" she asked. "Were you and Missy close?"

Cassie shook her head.

"No. But I supposedly was the last person to see her alive." She pointed toward the door. Beyond that was the hallway that led to the main coffee shop room. "She came to get a coffee a few hours before she was found beneath the bridge."

"You two talk?"

"Unlike the rest of the town, I thought it would have been impolite to ignore her. Or heckle her. We talked about the weather, about laptop brands, and then about how expensive whipped cream had gotten. She left when she was done with her coffee. She tipped well, smiled nice, and then was just gone. That's the long and short of it."

"Laptop brands?" That wasn't exactly normal chatter, especially with Cassandra, who had never been a fan of technology in school.

"She had one with her and seemed capable enough with it. I asked if she liked it well enough since my youngest, Hunter, spilled milk all over mine and I needed to get another. She was nice about that too."

Talking about laptops, the weather, and whipped cream hours before potentially jumping off a bridge. Drinking coffee too. It didn't sound like a woman who was planning not to see the end of the day.

Then again, not everyone was so cut and dry with their actions.

Cassandra pushed back in her chair but didn't stand. It seemed she had finally reached the end of her patience.

"You can tell your sheriff that that's all I know and that's all we did. Past that, I'm not going to talk about Missy again. He's the one who signed off on the end of her case in the first place. He needs to let it go and move on, like the rest of town. That goes for you too, Blake. Don't go poking your nose around me or mine."

Her words were harsh.

Blake respected them.

She selected another candy from the dish and nodded.

"I can take him with me now, but I'll never make it out of the shop if Corrie is still waiting for me," she pointed out.

Cassandra picked up her cell phone and typed a message out for a bit.

Then she pointed back to the door.

"I called her off. You can leave now and she won't bother you."

Blake chuckled.

"If only I could have that power over my sister."

The thought slipped out before Blake even realized she'd had it. All humor vanished. She tried to overcompensate and gave her old friend a smile and pivoted back to an earlier thought.

"So, why didn't you just talk to the sheriff about all this?" Blake asked. "It doesn't seem like any information that was worth dodging the law for."

Cassandra seemed to consider her answer for a moment. Her lips twisted a little before she spoke, like she was regretting it before she said a word.

"Word got around that the sheriff was asking questions about Missy even after everything was finished up. It really upset her dad, but it struck even more sour with those old goons who still worship him from their time at the supply. You know, the ones who started working there in their teens and managed to retire before he sold it off?" She shook her head. "It might have been nothing that I told you, but if it got around that I said that nothing to the sheriff, I might get some looks I don't want."

"Ah." So there it was. "So now it's on me."

Cassandra didn't try to deny it.

"If it gets around town that you're talking about Missy to the sheriff, then that's on you. Even if they find out I'm the one who told you, it's still on you."

Blake snorted. She wasn't mad at the intention. In fact, she understood it.

"Whoever says that Corrie is the scarier twin hasn't met the real you."

But Blake smiled true.

"It was good to see you, Cassie," she added. "I'm glad you're doing well. Truly."

Cassandra didn't return the smile, but she did nod.

It wasn't until Blake was one foot out of the door that she called out to her.

"Hey, Blake, I'm sorry about Beth."

Blake paused.

"Me too."

Blake refocused her attention as she made her way back to the main dining room. On the way, she passed Corrie. The woman was scowling but also silent. She met Blake's eye with a barely contained sneer and was gone right after.

Then there was Liam.

Blake stopped next to their table. She handed him the candy in her hand.

"I'm not in the mood for coffee anymore, so how about we do dinner tonight instead?"

LIAM WAS STARING into his closet. Theo was inside and sporting a brown blazer that had only seen the world twice since being purchased at a strip mall in Florida. The teen flapped his arms, then did another twirl.

"This isn't the worst thing you own," he said. "It actually looks pretty decent, good with your jeans too." Theo made a show of looking him up and down. "Unless you want to change into something else."

Liam almost rolled his eyes. He avoided the urge. Theo

had been in his apartment for less than a half hour and, in that time, had already made several jabs about his appearance.

"This isn't some kind of date," Liam said, once again. "I'm just going out to dinner. I don't need to dress up any more than this."

Theo didn't hold back his urge to roll his eyes.

"You're finally doing something social after business hours. With a woman." He shrugged. "I feel like that's as close to a date as you're going to get. Why not make more of an effort?"

"Says the guy who refuses to say hi to his crush of, what did you say, five years?"

That seemed to hit home. Theo took off the blazer. Liam pointed to the hanger.

"Hey, I'm just trying to help a divorced man get his groove back." He hung the blazer back up. "That's not a crime. That's *charity*."

"That's sticking your nose where it doesn't belong," Liam corrected. He backtracked through his bedroom to the kitchen. His badge was on the counter, his cell phone next to it.

Fifteen more minutes until he would be leaving.

Fifteen more minutes until he would be meeting Blake at the restaurant.

"Plus, this isn't remotely a date. This isn't even a social call. It's about work."

Liam said it with a little too much vigor. Maybe he was trying to underline the reason he had agreed to Blake's invitation for himself too.

"After work hours though?" Theo prodded. "Do you know how rare that is for you? Sheriff No Work Talk After Clocking Out. You can't expect me not to question this. Unless there's something *else* going on."

"There's nothing else going on. Blake just has a busy

schedule I'm trying to accommodate. It's not like turning down Deputy Gavin for some beers when he wants to complain about the medical examiner hurting his pride."

Theo crossed his arms over his chest. He still looked skeptical.

"You met her for coffee this morning, you're going to dinner with her tonight. What's next?" he asked. "Staying at her house until morning?"

The boy cracked a grin.

Liam made sure to be stern.

"Don't even joke about that," he warned. "One word like that gets out, and all our ears are going to be filled with gossip that will most definitely put me in a mood. A mood that locks that front door, and that fridge, from a no-good, talkative teen."

Theo rolled his eyes again but then caught whatever snarky remark he was about to say. Instead, he put his hands up in mock surrender.

"I won't make a peep about your nighttime *work* meeting with the beautiful, and rumored to be single, Miss Bennet at the fanciest restaurant in town. My lips are officially sealed."

So, she *was* single.

Liam hadn't asked and hadn't planned on it either.

But now, he knew.

"Good," Liam said to the boy's promised silence. "I'll grab you a plate to eat tomorrow if you don't say another word about it, starting now."

Theo mocked a loud gasp. Then he bowed.

"I won't tell a soul you even left the complex. Much appreciated."

This time Liam did roll his eyes.

"Your mom said she won't be home until tomorrow night, so you can crash here. But you better not stay up too late. I know school is boring for a smarty like you, but that doesn't mean you're allowed to sleep through it. Got it?"

Theo saluted him.

"There's food in the fridge. Lock the door behind me."

Theo was fast. As soon as the door was closed behind him, Liam heard the dead bolt slide into place. Knowing Theo, this wouldn't be the end of date-talk between the two of him. It should have grated on Liam, but he was finding that Blake Bennet continually popping up on his radar didn't exactly bother him. However, it was starting to bother him when other people forced her to surface.

While Blake had excused herself to the bathroom at the coffee shop—which Liam now knew was her sneaking away to talk to Cassandra herself—Corrie Daniels had tried her best to grill him about the woman. She had been fishing without even throwing her own line in.

Liam hadn't fallen for it.

After her second mention of Ryan's name and his sudden reappearance in town, Liam had done something he very rarely did.

He had made small talk.

The weather came first, then the coffee shop and how business was doing.

Liam had stayed in those conversations with his feet dug in and resolution clear.

Maybe that's why Corrie had been so quick to leave once she had gotten a text on her phone.

Or, maybe, whoever was texting had way more power than he did over the woman.

Either way, she had gone and Blake had come back... different.

It was why he had agreed to her dinner invitation so quickly.

He wanted to know what Cassandra had said, sure, but he wanted to know why it had changed Blake.

So he got into his truck and pointed it in the direction of the restaurant she had picked. The streetlamps outside of the apartment complex gave way to the dark of night while the stretch between residential and commercial held nothing but road, dirt, and trees.

The song on the radio belted out some catchy beat with a guy crooning about love.

He was still singing when Liam found his way back to the light, and the song was still going when Liam saw the woman of the hour standing outside of the restaurant, waiting for him.

Her hair was braided. Her blouse was red. Her jeans looked nice.

Her smile, when she saw him, was warm.

Blake Bennet might have been Sheriff Trouble in the past, but right then and there, she was simply one thing to Liam.

Breathtaking.

Even when she was hustling to his window and motioning for him to roll it down.

She didn't waste any time in her request.

"I only had your office number or else I would have called, but is there any way we could change locations?" She dove in. "Bruce kind of destroyed the kitchen earlier and threw off our family schedules. Lola is back at the house with him now, and I have Clem with me."

Liam finally saw the rolled-down window of the car behind her. The little girl from the daycare program was staring intently at them. She seemed calmer than her aunt, that was for sure.

"She's a good kid, but there's not a thing she'll eat off

the menu here. The diner, however, has some of her favorite chicken nuggets."

Blake's eyebrow rose. She didn't give him space to respond as she added, "Or we can reschedule? Or maybe I can just talk to you on the phone instead?"

Liam would later wonder if his answer would have been the same had someone else been asking. In the moment, however, his response was quick.

"I happen to be a chicken nugget fan myself. You lead the way and I'll follow."

Chapter Seven

The change of location had been a simple request, but Blake had found herself oddly nervous about it. No doubt Lola's parting speech hadn't helped.

"The fact that he already agreed to eat with you is a good sign that he won't mind Clem being there or y'all going to the diner," she had said over her mop and bucket. "I'm still surprised he said yes in the first place. Since he moved to town, that man hasn't been very social. Some think that's why he got his divorce, and some think he's closed off *because* of his divorce. Either way, he doesn't seem like the kind of man to get snobby about a kid or a change in plans."

Lola had shrugged.

"And if he makes a fuss, then fuss right on back," she'd added. "If that doesn't work, give me a call and Bruce and I will show up and fuss too. That'll teach him to get into a snit over nothing."

Blake had waved off the offer of the fussing backup, though she'd been touched. Not just anyone would go to bat against a sheriff for her.

Lola's words, as supportive as they were, however, had Blake antsier than she had anticipated when driving up to the restaurant.

She wanted to talk to Liam.

She wanted him to *want* to talk to her.

Maybe it was because he had helped her with Ryan. Maybe it was because they both understood what it meant to be a sheriff. Maybe it was because, other than Lola, he was the first adult in town not to ask the hard questions.

Talking to Liam had so far been an easy thing to do.

So when he was quick to assure her that their change of plans wouldn't make him leave, Blake couldn't help but feel some relief.

In fact, there was some excitement too.

"We're going to eat with an actual adult, Clem," she called over her shoulder once she was back in her car. "Someone who *doesn't* live in our house. That means we need to be on our best behavior. No yelling from me, no throwing food for you. We don't want to scare the sheriff off."

Clem was in a jumper covered in cartoon ducks. Her hair was braided and, in the right light, looked identical to Blake's. It was a point of pride for Blake that she was the only one Clem would let play with her hair. And play it had become since Blake learned quickly that doing her own hair in braids was one thing. Doing a toddler's hair in braids was another.

"You ready to go?" Blake asked the girl, reversing into position in front of Liam's truck. Surely he knew how to get to the diner, yet he was waiting for them. It was sweet.

Clem apparently agreed.

"He's gonna eat chicken nuggs too," she squealed in delight. Blake saw her wave in the truck's direction. She couldn't see if Liam waved back. "Chicken nuggs with ranch," Clem added once they were going forward again. "Ranch, ranch, ranch."

Blake laughed at that.

"You and your ranch. You know I told your grandma that

it might not be a bad idea to throw you a ranch-themed party for your next birthday."

Clem broke out into giggles.

"With chicken nuggs?" she asked between them.

Blake nodded.

"With chicken nuggs."

Clem started to talk about food some more, and Blake navigated the stretch between the restaurant's parking lot right out to the town's biggest collective grievance—the new intersection. One that Blake had only experienced a handful of times since coming back.

"It's like whoever added in that intersection was paid to make it as much as a pain in the tuchus as possible," Lola had once complained about the spot. "I went the wrong way twice there, and I don't even feel bad about it. None of it makes sense!"

Blake had done enough driving in enough less-than-ideal areas that the intersection didn't bother her as much. That didn't mean she let her guard down though. She was hyper-aware of the cars around them as she rolled to a stop. It's why she noticed that the vehicle behind her was not, in fact, the sheriff's truck.

"I guess Liam is one of those Sunday drivers," Blake mused aloud. "He probably let me lead because he likes taking his time behind the wheel."

The idea of someone as intimidating-looking as Liam being a passive driver really got into Blake's system. One more laugh and Clem caught on, and when the light changed to green both were giggling nonsense.

Blake's heart softened and squeezed all at once.

Beth should have been able to hear it too.

That ache bloomed.

Blake had never regretted her decision to leave Seven

Roads years ago. She hadn't regretted her choices after that either. Each step she had taken after crossing the town limits line was done with confidence and pride. Even the missteps. They had been hers and she had embraced them all.

She had created an unmovable foundation for her future.

It was only after coming back that she realized there had always been a crack that ran through it.

Beth.

The golden child. The baby of the family. The little sister who had made all the right choices in the eyes of their father while Blake had done everything wrong.

That's how she had seen Beth in her mind, even if she had convinced herself that she hadn't.

Beth, though, had never once said a word against her. She had supported each choice Blake had made, forced her to endure phone calls and video chats at least once a month, and had always kept her updated on her life. She had also always asked for updates from Blake's.

Their mother had left them. Their father had let Blake go.

Beth?

She had held on as best she could until she had been forced to leave too.

It wasn't until Blake was sitting in an attorney's office, holding a small note written in her sister's silly little handwriting that Blake had finally found the crack in her life. The one that would now forever be filled with regret.

If you're reading this, then I guess something not-so-great happened to me, the note had begun. *So let's skip the sad part and get to the nice. I love you, Blakey. Let my kids love you too. Take care of each other. And make sure to eat something yummy. Love, your sister, Beth.*

Regret. Grief. Immense sadness. Total love.

Just under fifty words in total and Blake felt everything all at once.

She was living in Beth's home, raising her children a week later.

Now, she knew Clem had a passion for ranch dressing that rivaled most epic love stories. That Bruce kicked his feet a little when he was content. That Clem didn't talk at all while watching TV but would sing the intro songs loudly and with delight as soon as the screen went dark. That Bruce happy-danced when his sister started her singing and became even louder when Lola joined in.

Blake had learned a lot of little things since she'd come home.

The biggest thing?

She missed her sister something fierce.

"Hey, Clem?" Blake said, clearing her throat to stave off tears she knew would come if she kept on with her current thoughts. Instead, she went to a happier memory. "Let me tell you about something your mama used to eat that ran me up the wall when we were kids."

They were moving along the access road that eventually would take them to the side of the diner. The lighting along the road consisted of exactly one outdated streetlamp. It left an orange glow in the dark across Clem's curious expression as Blake glanced at her in the rearview mirror.

The headlights coming up fast behind them cut through that glow with startling quickness.

Blake pressed the gas pedal down hard.

It was the only reason the approaching vehicle didn't rear-end them.

Adrenaline flooded her system, but Blake reserved her gut reaction to curse the driver. It was surely an accident. The driver probably wasn't paying attention. The alarms in her head going off had nothing to do with some kind of on-going danger.

Why would there be any here in Seven Roads, after all?

No sooner than she had the thought than it vanished.

The headlights became bigger as the car behind them sped up again.

Blake didn't leave room for interpretation now.

The car was trying to hit them.

And there was no time to figure out why.

"Hold on, Clem."

A DRIVER WENT when they weren't supposed to at the head-ache of an intersection. Once they realized their mistake, they panicked and stopped in the middle of the street. Blake and the car that had been able to slip in between her and Liam had managed to get ahead of the confusion. Liam, however, rolled down his window and slowed next to it.

He recognized the older woman behind the wheel and motioned for her to roll her window down too.

She did so, eyes wide.

Liam cut off any lengthy explanation or apology.

"It's okay, Mrs. Connie," he called out. "The light changes here don't make much sense. Just try to be more careful. You can go on now."

She had been trying to turn into the same lane as he was in, so Liam waved her ahead, glad that they were the only cars around.

Mrs. Connie wasn't so sure, so he called out to her again and told her to go ahead with more assurances.

She did so after a few more moments that seemed to crawl by. Not everyone became nervous around Liam, but Mrs. Connie always acted as though she'd been on the fence about law enforcement. Her overcautiousness showed as Liam's speed was reduced by twenty following her down the two-lane road.

He sighed and accepted the delay. Blake's taillights were nowhere in sight. He idly wondered how people had treated her during her times as a sheriff. She had left a small town that hadn't known her originally and yet she'd managed to be elected during her time living there.

It was the same as his story, but Liam would bet money that Blake had blazed her way into her position. He, on the other hand, had been elected for McCoy County's sheriff in a calm, quiet event. There had been no pushback, no fuss that he wasn't a true local. There had simply been a need for the position to be filled after the former sheriff had retired. Liam just so happened to be there with the right résumé.

He had been suspicious though at first. Why hadn't someone else tried to run against him?

Price had been open about the answer.

"We're boring here in McCoy County," he'd said. "Not a bad thing, but there's not many people who want to be in charge of all of that boring."

Boring equated to still. Still meant quiet.

Liam started to knead his hip with his fist.

Quiet is what he'd been wanting.

The current silence in the cab of his truck didn't last long. It was only humorous timing that a few moments after recalling his memory with Price did his name pop up on the phone screen.

It was just past seven. Both men were off work.

Liam answered with an eyebrow raise that no one could see.

"Hello?"

Price's words came out through the truck's speakers strong but rushed.

"Where are you right now?"

Liam's back zipped straight to attention.

"Just left the cluster intersection. Running along the access road that goes to County 22. Why?"

Mrs. Connie was still going too slow. It now made Liam feel anxious.

What Price asked next didn't help matters.

"Can you see Blake?"

Both hands went to the steering wheel.

"No. Why?"

Price was moving. Rustling came through the line.

"She just called me saying someone is trying to drive her off the road," he hurried out. "She can't get your business card while she's defensive driving, so I'm sending her contact now. She said she needs your help."

Liam flipped on his hazards. His phone made an additional beep.

The text came in fast.

Liam was faster.

He was already passing Mrs. Connie when he clicked the number link.

"Hang up with me and get out here," Liam ordered.

Price didn't respond. The call ended.

Liam hit the call button on the new number.

It rang once before Blake answered.

The road noise coming through the call was startling loud.

"Liam?" she asked before he could say a word.

His name had never made him sit at such attention before.

"I'm here."

That's all Blake seemed to need. She launched into the situation with notable calm.

"Some four-door car—I can't tell the make—has been trying to run us off the road. They already managed to bump me at the turn. I— Hold on, Clem." She cut herself off and filled in the space with some cussing.

Liam's grip tightened on the wheel and his foot pushed the gas pedal down hard.

The access road's end was in the distance. She would have had to turn left toward town or right, taking her along County 22. He needed to know where she went but only managed a quick question.

"Which way?"

Thankfully, she understood.

"County 22."

Clem was making noise, but he couldn't tell if she was just talking or crying. Blake's voice was strained as she continued.

Liam readied to make the right turn.

"I'm not going to go on the offense because Clem's in the car. I can't chance us wrecking. I'm guessing you're not too far behind me. Can you—"

"I'll end this," he promised. "Getting on County 22 now."

His tires squealed a little, his heart was pounding a lot.

Blake cussed again. Clem started clearly crying.

"We're going too fast." Blake was talking fast too. "If I go any faster and they hit us again, we'll crash. I—I don't think you're going to get to us in time. We've been flying since I got on here."

Liam was filling with anger.

He should have never let any car get between them.

"How much of the road do you have left?" he asked. His speedometer was topping out. If County 22 hadn't been a straight shot, he wouldn't have been able to do it as quickly. That was probably why Blake was confident that her and her tail were already so far ahead of him.

"The curve near Becker Farm's back end is coming up.

If he hits us, we'll flip." Blake's voice drastically changed. "We can't do that, Liam."

He'd only known her for two days, and yet Liam understood that the panic he heard was rare for the woman.

It pulled at every part of him.

Especially since he couldn't help her yet.

And even more so since the advice he was about to give her was less than ideal.

"Don't take the curve then," he said. "Hit the field to the left of it. It's flat, just mowed last week. Reduce speed enough that the entry won't rock you too hard. It'll force him to slow down too. If they even decide to follow."

If she didn't agree with the plan, there wasn't time to come up with another.

She agreed.

"Okay. Clem? Clem. I need you to hold on to your seat. Okay?"

Liam was running the math. He was a minute behind them, give or take. He could get there in thirty seconds if he didn't reduce his own speed. Clem's crying quieted.

"I don't have a weapon with me, Liam." Blake's voice had changed again. It was back to being hard. "You have until the field runs out to save us."

Liam felt straight fire in his veins.

"Yes, ma'am."

Chapter Eight

Blake pressed the brakes enough to drop their speed to keep them from wrecking as soon as the tires hit the grass shoulder. Every part of her was clenched, her knuckles white on the steering wheel. Her back so straight it wasn't even touching the seat.

She didn't have time to look back at Clem, but the silence in the car was astonishing. She had listened to Blake.

Blake hoped her promise to the girl that they would be okay would hold true.

The only break in focus from the field lasted long enough to see if the car followed them off the road.

Once she confirmed it did, Blake became single-minded.

They weren't going to crash.

That meant handling the field first.

The old Becker Farm had the most acreage in Seven Roads. The back end was part of that land but was notorious for never being used for anything practical. Mostly because Abe Becker didn't like being so close to a well-traveled road. Still, Abe was a proud man and kept every bit of his land maintained, especially the parts that were visible to the public.

Blake could have kissed the man for his decision.

The field was flat enough and freshly mowed, as Liam had said. Blake's car hit the grass without any dips or rises taking out her tires or crunching her bumper. That didn't mean the car was handling the change in terrain all that well.

The speedometer was at forty miles per hour when they went in, and she had to drop even farther the deeper they went.

Everything rattled.

Clem's quiet lasted a few yards in and then she was crying again.

The car chasing them followed but had to drop their speed just as fast. It made Blake's stomach drop. She'd been hoping that whatever the driver had wanted from them wouldn't continue with the added trouble.

She was wrong.

"Did you make it?" Liam's voice could barely be heard over the sound of the field beating against the car that dared run through it.

"Yeah," Blake yelled out. "They did too." She looked down at the speedometer again. "I'm slowing but we're going to hit the tree line sooner rather than later. Where are—"

The call dropped. Blake heard the familiar beep sound play through the car's speaker. The spotty service that Seven Roads's more rural areas usually sported had finally claimed their call.

It couldn't have happened at a worse time.

"We're—we're okay," Blake yelled back to Clem, trying to be as soothing as possible. The truth was they sounded like they were in a tin can during a tornado. The darkness around them made it even more terrifying. As an adult it wound Blake's nerves tight.

But now wasn't the time to worry about their feelings.

The tree line that ended the field was near the edge of the bouncing headlight beams.

There was no way she could keep driving once she got there.

She was going to have to turn and hope the car didn't—

The headlights behind them shifted. Blake watched in the rearview as the car behind them seemingly lost control. It took a hard right.

She didn't waste the breakaway.

Blake turned left with every intention of driving along the tree line before going back to the main road. But a horrifying sound followed by an awful shuddering changed that plan quick.

"Hold on, Clem!"

The front right tire didn't just blow. It exploded.

Blake felt it through the floorboard.

It was the nail in the coffin of her plan to flee.

She let off the gas pedal and held on to the steering wheel for dear life.

The next moment felt like it stretched hours when really it must have been only a few seconds. The car wobbled violently until coming to a stop a few feet from massive oak trees.

Blake whipped her head around to look out of the back windshield.

The pursuing car must have also been disabled. It was stopped a few yards diagonal to them. Without waiting to see what the driver did next, Blake made a split-second decision.

She tore her seat belt off and threw open her door. She repeated the sequence in reverse as she hurried to get Clem out of her car seat. The girl didn't fight her, but her sobbing pushed against Blake's chest when she had her out and against her.

"Wrap your legs around me," she told the girl firmly. "We're going to run now."

No sooner than she said it did Clem follow the directive. Her little arms wound around Blake's neck just as her legs fastened around Blake's waist. The added weight would make her slow, but Blake could at least gain enough distance to maybe turn the tables and ambush whoever followed.

If they followed. Maybe wrecking was enough to deter the driver?

A new terrifying sound broke through the night.

A car door opened.

Then another.

Blake didn't mean to—she couldn't afford the time—but she turned around.

Sure enough, two people had exited the car that had been chasing them.

Two men.

And one was holding something in his hand.

Clem's sobs racked Blake's body.

There was nothing between them and the men if they decided to run and attack them—if they decided to shoot.

Blake's mind tried to come up with solutions. What-ifs in which she kept Clem out of harm's way, but everything seemed to stall.

For the first time in her life, Blake felt immeasurable fear.

Her grip on Clem tightened.

It was why she didn't register the new set of headlights right away.

By the time she understood what she was seeing, the truck shuttered to a violent stop right between the cars. It effectively cut off Blake's view from the men.

It didn't keep her from seeing the new driver.

Or hearing him.

"Hands up or I'm shooting!"

Liam's voice was the loudest thing she had ever heard. It

echoed through the field and bounced back from the trees behind her.

His passenger-side window must have been open. His arm was raised and, she assumed, a gun in his hand aimed at the men. He didn't break his focus even as he got out. Instead, he kept his arm straight and trained on the men over the hood of the truck, adjusting as he went around it.

"Do it now!" he roared.

It was enough to get Blake moving again. She ran around her car to put another barricade between Clem and the men just in case they decided to resist.

A siren started blaring in the distance.

Another long second stretched by.

Whether it was because of backup coming or Liam's command, the men must have decided that resisting wasn't a good idea.

Blake could hear Liam going through the normal directions for apprehending suspects. His tone notably less aggressive as he did so.

Relief poured through Blake at the change.

She rubbed at Clem's back and spoke softly into the girl's hair as she hugged her tight.

"We're okay now," she said. "The sheriff is here."

THE MCCOY COUNTY SHERIFF'S DEPARTMENT showed up in fine force. Price came in first, followed by Deputy Mel Gavin, who had been nearby with his cruiser when Price had rallied the troops, and then in third had been Darius Williams, the ace—and only—detective in Seven Roads. However, he was the first person to identify the two men Liam had on the ground after their arrival.

Now, nearly two hours later and currently standing opposite Liam in a hallway at the sheriff's department, Detective Williams went into more depth about who they were.

"Chase and Ray McClennan are the youngest two of the McClennan families still living in town. They're cousins. Cousins who, up until now, haven't taken a step out of line in regards to the law. No criminal history. No nasty rumors. Just two good, average young twentysomethings who've been around town since they were born."

Liam cussed as big as an elephant. He would have curbed the urge if Blake and Clem were in the room with him, but both were sitting in his office a few doors down, Price with them, until Liam finished up. Until he was in the same space again, he let his anger flare.

"They chased down a woman and her child at night in the middle of nowhere. While one of them was holding." Liam shook his head. "They could be heaven-picked saints before this, and it wouldn't change how much I want to wring their necks. They didn't give you any idea why they went after Blake?"

Darius shook his head now.

"Ray just repeated what he'd already told you when you were handcuffing him in the field," he said. "'We got the wrong car. We thought it was our friend's and wanted to mess around.'"

Liam snorted at the direct quote. The older one, who he'd find out later was Ray, had been the one to spout that nonsense.

"Do you believe that?" he asked Darius.

The detective didn't nod but also didn't shake his head.

"Considering I couldn't get them to tell me what friend they thought it was, I'm thinking they aren't being truthful about it. I can't say for sure yet since I didn't get much else from them before they were hollering for a lawyer." He flipped his wrist over to see the face of his watch. "It's too late to talk to them tonight. I'll have to wait until the morning. You want to be in there with me?"

Liam wanted nothing more than to get the truth from the cousins. He gave the detective a reserved "Yes" but could still feel himself boiling.

From the time their phone call had cut out to seeing both cars stopped in the field, Liam had felt utterly helpless. When he'd gotten close enough to see that the men were outside of the car staring at Blake? He'd felt worry replace it.

When he'd seen the gun that Ray had been holding? Anger had come into play.

When he'd heard that baby girl crying for all she was worth after they had secured Ray and Chase in handcuffs? Liam had seen absolute red.

He wanted the cousins to explain themselves.

If they were lying, he wanted to know why.

And he wanted to know the absolute truth so he could make sure it would never happen again.

"I'll be back first thing in the morning," Liam added before they parted ways. "Don't start without me."

Darius said he wouldn't and left.

Next was Liam's office. He took a beat before entering, checking his anger at the door. At least, any traces of it. He was glad for the chance. As soon as he walked through the door, all eyes were on him.

All eyes that were awake.

Clem was fast asleep against Blake, both sitting on the love seat against the far wall. Price was cleaning up food wrappers from their fast-food supper. Not that the adults had eaten all that much. Clem, however, had stopped crying at the sight of chicken nuggets. Liam wasn't experienced with little kids, but he thought that was less of an age thing and more of a comfort thing.

She'd just been through a lot and had been scared and confused.

Just like the woman currently giving him a wide-eyed stare.

Liam lowered his voice and motioned to the door.

"If you're ready, I'll take you two home now."

Blake looked like she wanted to ask every question she had right then and there, but Clem shifted against her. That look turned to acceptance.

"I just finished my statement, so we're good to go."

She started to stand. It was an effort with the sleeping girl in her arms. The same sight had met him when he had finally been able to check on them after Ray and Chase were dealt with. Clem was glued to her aunt and her aunt wasn't complaining.

That didn't mean she didn't need help.

Liam stood in front of them and leaned over, arms outstretched.

"Let me carry her to the truck," he said.

Blake was quick to decline.

"It's okay. I can—"

Liam fixed her with a level stare and interrupted with an excuse.

"I need your hands free so you can set up the car seat," he said. "So help me out and let me carry her."

Blake was exhausted. He could see it in every part of her face. He could also hear it in her relenting.

"Okay. If you don't mind."

He didn't, and soon the three of them were walking slowly out to the parking lot. Lightning forked in the distance and the breeze had taken on some moisture. Still, the world was quiet around them.

They didn't disturb that silence.

Blake set up the baby seat in the back seat of his truck while Liam moved slightly side to side. Clem kept sleeping, warm against his chest. She didn't wake when he transferred her into the seat and stayed just as asleep as he started driving.

It was only after Blake had finished giving directions to her home that Liam repeated what Darius had told him about the McClennan cousins. Blake was as unimpressed with their answer as he was.

"We could have been seriously hurt, or worse, and that's all they're saying?" She actually snarled. "Do they not realize how serious this is? My sister died the same way, for goodness sake. And this time her child was in the car."

The parallel wasn't lost on him.

"We're talking to them again tomorrow, first thing," he said. "Don't worry. Whether they thought you were someone else or not, they're definitely about to learn a hard lesson."

Blake nodded. A few moments later she sighed.

"I should have just told you about my conversation with Cassandra at the café this morning instead of dragging it out," she said. "But I guess I got that feeling again and wanted to make it last as long as I could."

Liam didn't take his eyes off the road but inclined his head a little at that.

"That feeling?"

Out of his periphery, he could see her tap the upper part of her chest.

"Working a case, chasing justice, that kind of feeling," she answered. "I've been out of the game for half a year, and sometimes it feels like a whole life slipped away in between. Still, dragging out your investigation into a girl who died just to play pseudo sheriff again was cruel of me. I'm sorry."

Liam hadn't expected that. Much like the panic in her voice earlier, the sheer defeat that he heard in her words caught him off guard. The walls that Blake Bennet must have had around her dropped away for the second time that night.

He didn't like that she had to do it alone.

"I'm the one who should be apologizing," he said. "I'm sure Cassandra told you about what happened with Missy and how the case is closed—and that I closed it—but now can't let it go. The truth is, I've been going off only one thing that doesn't add up and a gut feeling. I shouldn't have pulled you into that. We both know how dangerous it can be to become obsessed over a case."

But that didn't mean he was going to let Missy's death go. Not until he was sure no one else had been involved. He wasn't going to admit that to the woman sitting next to him though. Blake had been through enough.

Her hair shifted in his periphery as she nodded.

Once again, he could see how tired she was. Her next words even came out in an air of quiet.

"They talked about whipped cream, laptop brands, and the weather. That was the long and short of it. Cassandra said Missy left after that." Blake laughed quietly. It had no humor in it. "This whole night could have been avoided if I'd said that earlier. No muss, no 'plowing through a field and terrifying my poor niece' fuss."

Liam should have consoled her once again. Reassured her that none of what had happened was her fault.

Yet he had gotten hung up on something.

"They talked about laptop brands?" he asked.

"Mm-hmm. Missy had hers at the counter and Cassandra was asking how she liked it since she needed to buy a new one and is notoriously bad at all technology. Missy was nice enough to answer."

Liam didn't respond.

The sound of Blake shifting in her seat had him guess that she had turned toward him.

"Why? Is there something there?"

Liam shook his head.

"There was nothing there."

Blake sighed out long.

"There was nothing there," she repeated, like the topic was done.

But for Liam it had just started.

"No," he said. "I mean we never found a laptop with Missy or with her belongings. There was nothing there."

This time he did glance at his passenger. Light from the approaching intersection showed him an expression that was all thoughtful.

"Then what happened to it between the café and the bridge?"

Liam didn't know, but he sure was going to try to find out.

Chapter Nine

Rain started to fall two steps after they were inside of the house. Once again Liam took charge of carrying Clem. If Blake hadn't called ahead to let Lola know they were coming, she was sure the older woman would have been shocked quiet at the sudden appearance of the big man holding their small kiddo.

Instead, she greeted them all at the door with a tight hug for Blake, a soft back rub for the sleeping Clem, and a little pat on Liam's arm. It wasn't until Clem had been settled in her room and all three adults were standing around the living room that Lola and Liam were officially introduced.

"I would have liked meeting you under better circumstances, but I have to say, Sheriff, I'm sure glad you were around." Lola reached out for Blake's hand. "When Blake called me earlier to tell me about what happened... I, well, I'm just really glad everything worked out the way it did."

Liam gave her a small smile. He waved his hand a little as if swatting away the nice.

"I didn't do much," he said. "Blake here is the one that did all the work. I just showed up at the end."

They all knew that wasn't true—Liam had put a stop to the madness—but it was late, and they weren't there to re-hash what had happened. Lola wasn't letting him go that fast though. While Blake and Clem had eaten takeout at the sheriff's department, Liam hadn't had one bite. Once Lola realized he had an empty stomach, her Southern manners refused to let him leave.

"I'm making you an egg-and-bacon scramble," she announced. "Unless you really want to fight me on it, why don't the two of you go take the weight off your poor feet?" Lola caught Blake's eye. "The chairs are ready."

The sheriff raised his eyebrow at that.

"The chairs?"

Blake led the way back outside to the front porch. She motioned to the random assortment of outdoor chairs lined up next to the railing. There were two adult-sized and one miniature chair, covered in rainbows. Around those were a few wayward dinosaur figurines, an empty can of Play-Doh, two bottles of bubbles, and a smattering of shoes lined haphazardly along the wall.

"We're a family who really likes to watch the rain," Blake explained. She eyed the slight chaos that was around the chairs. "And apparently a family who forgets to clean the front porch. Sorry for the mess."

Liam settled into one of the chairs. He laughed.

Blake followed suit and settled in the chair next to him. The rain was still falling outside, but it was a soft shower. Soothing. Cool. Relaxing. At least as much as it could be considering the last few hours.

"It's not mess," he said. "It's breadcrumbs."

"Breadcrumbs?" Blake parroted.

She watched as the corner of Liam's lip turned up ever so slightly.

"A buddy of mine used to say the thing he missed the most about home while we were deployed were the breadcrumbs. You know, the little things people leave around their homes that prove a family lives there." He laughed. "He used to talk about the hair ties his daughter and wife would leave lying around everywhere. The cats would find them, eat them, and then cough them up, making a mess. He'd say he'd get up in the middle of the night for some water, and if he could make it to the fridge without stepping on one or the other, it was a win. Things like that. A chipped bowl no one ever throws away, discarded socks in random places, toys and books and the pen you can never find when you need it, but it's always in the way when you don't. His family called that breadcrumbs. You follow them, you'll find a family."

It was the most Liam had ever said to her in one go.

Which made the idea of breadcrumbs even more endearing to her.

"Breadcrumbs," she repeated. "I like that. It's a more charming way to call something messy, that's for sure. Though I'm not sure Lola would take breadcrumbs as a good excuse to skip cleaning day. That might be pushing my luck." Blake smiled at the thought. Liam caught it.

"You two seem really close. Lola, I mean. She lives here with you full time?"

Blake nodded.

"That's how we got close, to be honest," she admitted. "She's technically my stepmom. My dad married her after I'd already left town, so I'd only met her a few times before coming back to Seven Roads." Blake hesitated. She didn't want to unload any more sad family stories, so instead of detailing what had led Lola to move in with her, she decided to be brief. "She already had a good relationship with the kids and came to live with us to help out."

"Did your dad come too?"

It was a reasonable question. He didn't know that there had been a falling-out between her father and Blake when she was younger. He didn't know about the falling-out that had happened again after Beth's death.

So Blake didn't answer that in detail either.

"No. He lives in Alabama."

Whether he wanted to know more or simply took the hint, Liam accepted her answer as enough. Blake capitalized on that and switched back to an earlier subject.

"You texted Darius asking about Missy's laptop right after we got here, right? Did he respond yet?"

Missy having a laptop the day she died had indeed been news to Liam. After admitting he had never seen it, he'd sent a few messages to Darius after parking in her driveway. He'd buttoned up about it right after, focusing on getting Clem in the house. Blake had momentarily forgotten about the news the moment she had seen Lola's worried gaze.

And when they were tucking Clem in?

All Blake had been thinking about was how hard the girl had cried against her.

Now she had the space to backtrack, though the excitement from the morning at working a case had dulled. Blake wouldn't admit it, but she was exhausted. Physically and emotionally. Once Liam was done eating, she was going to check on Bruce and then probably lie down next to Clem on her bed for comfort.

Hers more than Clem's, if she was being honest.

Liam pulled his cell phone out but didn't check it. He nodded.

"He just confirmed that none of us saw a laptop," he said. "I told him we'd talk about it after we talk to the McClennan cousins tomorrow. We'll see if it was an oversight on our part."

"What do you think the alternative could be?"

The question popped out before she could stop it. Liam's expression went impassive.

"Sorry," she said. "Old habit."

Blake returned her gaze to the rain past the railing.

She was surprised when Liam didn't skip a beat in answering her.

"I don't think Missy jumped off that bridge voluntarily. I think something might have happened to get her there. That laptop might be the missing thing that either proves my hunch or finally puts it to rest."

Resolution, calm and clear, came through every word.

It was still strong as he snorted.

"It's been like pulling teeth to try to piece together Missy's last day. I've never run into so much resistance from an entire town."

Blake knew that feeling.

"That's an old Seven Roads habit right there," she said. "If one person thinks you're in the wrong, it won't be long before the whole town thinks it too. Especially if that one happens to be someone like Mr. Clearwater."

Liam turned to her. She gave him an apologetic look.

"Cassandra said you had his fans all up in arms by asking questions after the case closed."

He grumbled.

"I'll never understand how a retired businessman has so many folks sticking up for him. You'd think he was a celebrity or something."

"He might as well be one," Blake said. "Jobs are a big deal here. Some of those guys had been working at the tractor supply straight from high school up until retirement." She became angry again. "You know, Ray and Chase McClennan's fathers were like that. They started working at the tractor supply alongside Mr. Clearwater when they were all in their twenties. They managed to retire before he shut down the business. He kept them and their families fed and clothed for their entire lives basically. That's where the loyalty comes from."

That was also why Missy had taken the general public's criticism for her father's decision to sell the business. No one would go up against the elder Clearwater since they would potentially have to deal with those older folks who had been through thick and thin with her daddy.

It hadn't been fair to Missy.

"I wonder how they'll act when they find out what their kids did."

Blake shrugged.

"Not every parent will go to bat for their kids. They might come down harder on them than even you could. I don't know much about their dynamic, but I bet, regardless, they'll all be loud about it."

The door behind them opened right in time to stop their conversation. Lola presented Liam with her scramble bowl with a flourish. That flourish extended in part to Blake when she handed her a bag of little cookies.

"You earned it," she said, all smiles.

Blake let out a breath and returned the affection.

A year ago, she had barely known Lola. Now she couldn't imagine her not being around.

Blake's gaze fell onto the man next to her.

A week ago, he hadn't even been on her radar. Now? Would Blake be okay not seeing him again?

Blake decided not to think about any of that yet.

Instead, she listened to the rain with the sheriff at her side.

Chapter Ten

A week passed and nothing about it was satisfying.

Ray and Chase McClennan remained committed to their story. They had believed Blake was their friend Henry, driving a new car and messing with them. They had followed her into the field because they thought it was funny. Chase hadn't known about the gun Ray had in his hand, and Ray had been insistent that he had simply had it to give Henry a funny scare. If Ray hadn't had a permit for the gun, he would still be in jail. But both of them were now out and about.

It had absolutely riled Liam up.

That wasn't even figuring in the lack of laptop either. Liam had gone through every part of the original investigation again to try to find the computer that Missy had had at the coffee shop, but he had come up short. He was on the fence about reaching out to her father again to see if maybe he had any idea where it might have gone and was still thinking about it when Price knocked on his office door and let himself in.

"Winnie heard some talk at school about the McClennan boys," Price said, bypassing a traditional start to a new conversation. He sat down opposite him in a chair that squeaked at the weight.

"We're still talking about those two?" Liam asked, instantly grumpy. "Also, isn't your daughter in high school? What talk about the McClennan cousins are going around there?"

Price adopted a high-pitched, flitty voice.

"'Oh, Sheriff, haven't you *seen* Chase McClennan?'" He dropped into a more dramatic voice. "He's young enough that the high school girls think they might have a chance with him if they say just the right thing. He's also just old enough that flirting with him at the restaurant he works at has become the 'it' dare in the past few months. According to Winnie, Amber Bell even live-streamed her asking for his number. He declined. She was mortified."

Price said everything with a straight face. And with an absolute sincerity. Liam could always tell the difference when Price was talking about anything that had to do with Winnie, including the talk that she was simply relaying to him.

Price Collins loved his daughter immensely.

Liam didn't have children, but he couldn't deny that his deputy's dedication to his daughter made him appreciate the man more.

"So even the high school has its own rumor mill about the rest of us," Liam mused.

Price nodded to that.

"Based on what I've heard since Winnie started, it's way more vicious than this fluff we have out here." He sat straighter and leaned forward a little. "And they get some of theirs from eavesdropping on their parents, which makes the new theory floating around the school more interesting than it already is."

Liam couldn't help it. He leaned in a little too. "Theory?"

Price's retelling of the news he had heard from his daughter was delivered in his own voice this time.

"No one at that school thinks that the guys were going

after a friend but instead trying to mess with—drumroll please—you."

"Me?"

Price nodded.

"Apparently a lot of the parents have been talking and, when they found out Blake was helping you with looking into Missy's death, they all decided that Ray and Chase went after her to scare her off or maybe send you a message." Price held up his hands in defense before Liam could start in. "This is just what Winnie said she heard from a group of seniors. The word is that Blake went back to her old ways of being an outcast sheriff and teamed up with you, *another* outcast sheriff, to dig into the Missy thing."

Liam balled his fist.

"Why would they even care? Ray and Chase, I mean." He was trying very hard not to go on a tangent. "Were they friends with Missy?"

Price's expression tightened a bit. He was annoyed at his own words.

"I asked Winnie, and she said the only friend Chase ever really hangs around is Cooper Han. He's a senior, I've met him once or twice. Good kid, as far as I can tell, a whiz with computers too. Not exactly on brand for someone who might want to send the sheriff a threatening message. Ray was acquainted with Missy, but they never ran in the same social circles. But their fathers…"

Liam nearly growled. He remembered Blake's words from the week before when they were sitting out on the porch.

"They're fans of Jonathan Clearwater, Missy's dad," he finished.

Price nodded.

"Bingo," he said. "Winnie said she's heard the theory that Ray and Chase were following their dads' orders, or they were trying to win some points with them. Both men have been pretty vocal about you being a problem since word got around that you were still investigating on the sly."

Liam took the pen he had in his hand and slammed it down on the desktop.

"This is absolutely ridiculous," he said.

"It's also just a bundle of rumors from teenagers who were eavesdropping on adults, probably just shooting the breeze to pass the time. Either way, it doesn't look good on the boys' intelligence." He held up two fingers. "If their story about thinking they were messing with a friend is true, that was an absolutely ridiculous plan. If the story about them trying to mess with you and Blake because of the Missy investigation? Well, that's a special kind of stupid if you ask me."

Liam had to agree with that.

"I think Blake is the kind of woman who digs her heels in when someone tries to make her stop doing something she wants to do," Liam added after a moment. He shook his head. "That would have been a really bad plan on their part for sure."

Price nodded his agreement. Then he was all sighs.

"I know Seven Roads is a small town, but when you start seeing how everyone is connected, it sure feels smaller." He stood and stretched. "Either way, I thought you should hear what's going around. I'm not sure it holds any water, but I wanted you to know just in case. I'm heading out for now, though, unless you need me for something else."

"I appreciate it, but, no, I'm good here."

A smile stretched wide across Price's face.

"Good. I'm doing a movie night with Winnie, and those have become rare since she hit teenagehood. You have any plans on this fine Friday, Sheriff?"

Liam motioned to the paperwork piled in his inbox tray.

"You're looking at it."

Price whistled, already moving to the door.

"Give me a deputy's badge over a sheriff's any day."

He left with a laugh. Liam went back to his paperwork. However, his attention strayed once again.

Had the McClennan cousins really tried to use Blake to shake them away from looking into Missy? Did their fathers' loyalty to Missy's father really run so deep that the children would risk such harsh consequences?

And why go after Blake and not him directly?

Unless Ray had simply pulled up behind the wrong car and had meant to target him instead.

This wasn't helping his hunch that something had happened to Missy that led to her death. If she really had taken her own life, then why was there this much resistance to his investigation?

And what about the flash drive?

Liam looked down at the locked drawer of his desk.

As far as he knew, only two people knew about the flash drive he had found under the bridge. Price and his friend who had analyzed the information he had found on the drive.

It was the main reason his gut wouldn't let her death go.

Liam had almost told Blake about the flash drive that night out on the porch. Instead, he'd stopped himself. Then he'd told her he could handle it alone.

And a week had gone by with no word from her.

Not that he could say a thing about that. He hadn't reached out either.

Liam glanced at his cell phone on the desk. He could send her a text to see how she was? To see how Clem was doing? How Bruce and Lola were too?

As if he willed it, his cell phone lit up right before it started to vibrate.

It wasn't Blake's number. It was Theo's, and he said just about the only thing that would make Liam leave his work behind without hesitation.

"Hey there, boss." Theo was whispering. "I just thought you should know there's a woman and a baby in your apartment right now. The lady's looking for you, and if I'm being honest, I don't think she's doing too hot."

BLAKE'S HEAD FELT like a vise was squeezing it. She blamed sinus pressure. She squinted through the pain at a picture frame on the TV stand. She was standing in Liam's apartment and staring at a photo in a nice wooden frame.

It was easy to find Liam at first glance. Among the group of men in the picture, he was the tallest. A tree among weeds. If Blake had felt better, she would have laughed at her own analogy at that. Instead, she traced the weeds with her eyes. Six men in total, all in varying stages of laughter. They were in military uniforms, but it looked to her like basic training rather than active deployment. Each man, Liam included, was covered in mud. Liam had some on his cheek. It made the gigantic smile on his face all the more charming.

Blake couldn't help but wonder when the last time he smiled like that was.

Maybe he was always that happy-go-lucky, but it was just reserved for certain people.

Maybe there was a special woman who did it for him too.

A thought that only popped into Blake's head after she had knocked on the sheriff's apartment door. It wasn't like they had talked about their personal lives that much. Apart from scanning his ring finger, she hadn't inquired about a wife, girlfriend or anyone else in that relationship realm.

You're only here to tell him something, not interrogate him, she had reminded herself while waiting for the door to unlock. Though bringing a baby probably wasn't a move she should have taken. Clem was at home doing crafts with Lola and Blake had to admit the situation last week had given her all kinds of feelings about the kids. She'd been sleeping with Clem, and anytime Bruce was near, she felt the urge to pull him up into her arms.

When she realized she wanted to loop Liam into her new little plan, she scooped Bruce up without a second thought. He'd even giggled when a teenager had opened the door with wide eyes.

After Theo had introduced himself, he'd been quick to cut off the questions popping up one after the other from her.

"I'm not his kid, by the way," he had exclaimed. "I live in the apartment complex. Liam lets me hang out here when my mom's working."

Bruce had trilled in delight at a new face, while Blake had spied a full meal on a plate at the table behind the teen. She also noted his shoes by the door and what appeared to be another set of the same size shoes next to them. There was a book bag too, slung on the couch arm. A cell phone was on top of it. He excused himself to make a call to Liam.

Theo had seemingly marked Liam's apartment as a safe space. It had warmed Blake's heart.

Now her heart did a little flutter as the dead bolt on the front door slid open. Bruce swiveled hard enough that Blake's balance tipped. Her head swam as she took a step to keep herself right. The ache around her head pulsed.

Sinuses.

That's all it was.

The door was open, and Liam was frowning. Blake pulled on a smile she hoped would defuse it. Theo spoke before either of them could.

"Wow, boss, you made some good time," he said. "You

must have broken some of those speeding laws you were supposed to be keeping good."

Liam's gaze slid to the boy's.

"And you must be done with all of your schoolwork?" Liam motioned to a door that must have been the second bedroom. "Why don't you go check?"

Theo raised his hands in defense but laughed. He gave a deep nod to Blake and scooped up his book bag.

"And on that note, I'll give y'all some space."

Blake felt bad for her intrusion and making the boy leave the living space, but at the same time, she didn't want him to listen to what she had to say.

"It was nice meeting you," she returned. Her smile was nothing compared to Bruce's. He did a little dance when Theo waved.

Then it was just the three of them in the living room.

Blake took a deep breath as dark eyes settled on hers.

There was no point in beating around the bush.

"I did something that you're not going to like."

Chapter Eleven

Blake was holding Bruce so that the boy was facing Liam. He started to babble, waving a toy in his hand, but neither adult was in a playful mood.

Liam didn't understand why Blake had shown up to his house with Bruce at night after a week of silence. There was also no diaper bag with her. Like she'd had to come there in a hurry.

Her statement definitely wasn't making him feel at ease.

What had gone wrong?

"What am I not going to like?" Liam asked.

Green eyes were locked on him and him only, but the sigh that escaped Blake's lips seemed to be for the entire world. She held up her free hand in a *Stop* gesture.

"Before you go scolding me, let me get everything out first, and then you have carte blanche on telling me I'm wrong. Okay?"

Liam felt his eyes narrow. He nodded still.

"Okay."

There was no more sighing after that. Blake dove in and didn't stop once.

"I know you said you'd handle it by yourself, but I've spent the last week looking for Missy's laptop, and I think I have a bead on it. After I started thinking about it and how this town really doesn't seem to be on your side about looking into Missy's death, I decided that I could at least just poke around a little to see if I could get something you couldn't. Specifically about the laptop. Since I don't know what all you've done in the primary investigation, I went to the coffee shop and heard that your talk with Missy's ex was less than helpful."

Kyle Langdon, Missy Clearwater's ex-boyfriend.

"Less than helpful" was an understatement. Liam had interviewed Missy's ex and had been thoroughly ticked at his behavior. Kyle had shown signs of being truly upset at her death but seemed to have no remorse for the possibility that his cheating scandal with Missy's best friend had contributed to her supposed leap off the haunted bridge. The man had instead acted as if he had done nothing wrong at all.

"We broke up for the greater good," was what he had said when Liam asked about the breakup. "Some things you just can't see eye to eye on, and there's nothing you can do about it."

It had been an off-putting response.

If Kyle hadn't had an airtight alibi of working at the steel mill during the window of time surrounding Missy's death, with security footage to confirm it, Liam would have bet money that he had been out on the bridge with Missy. The same went for Missy's former best friend, Miranda. She had said only a few words to Liam, and of those words, none of them had been regret or guilt.

They were sorry Missy had died, but they didn't believe their actions had had anything to do with it.

"Kyle doesn't know me," Blake continued. "So when I *casually* bumped into him and mentioned I had just moved to town, he got really chatty and weirdly accepting. That led to him inviting me out tomorrow. He was shooting for dinner, I switched it to afternoon coffee."

Liam broke his deal and broke his silence.

"You're not going."

Liam heard the hammer drop in his own words.

Blake paused at it. Green eyes searched his expression. It gave him enough time to edit himself.

"I don't like that man," he said, trying not to physically bristle at the idea. "There's something about him that rubs me the wrong way. Also inviting someone he just met out to dinner? That's another mark against him in my opinion."

Blake's eyebrow rose up.

"Didn't I ask you out and you agreed to dinner right after we met?"

Liam didn't have to think even once on that one.

"We're different," he defended. "This Kyle guy isn't me or you. I don't want you to go out with him."

He meant every word of what he said, Liam realized. He didn't like the idea of Blake sitting across from the man, dressed nice and smiling. It grated on him.

Blake blew out a huff. Bruce caught her finger as she tried to motion to him.

"That's why I'm here," she said. "I want to be bait. I figure we can do the same thing we did with Cassandra at the coffee shop. I'll sit down with him, ask a few questions, and then you can swoop in."

"Swoop in," he repeated. "I doubt he'll tell me anything else, even if you're there."

She shook her head.

"No, I mean swoop in to take *me* away. Not try to talk to him again."

It was such a simple request and she said it with such ease.

"I'll take you away," he repeated again.

Blake was unfazed.

"Yeah, but do it in a way that doesn't make him think we trapped him," she added. "Maybe don't wear the badge. Just, you know, come over and say we have plans later, and I'll just go with you. Like we have a date or something."

Liam's eyebrow went high of its own volition.

For the first time since they had met, Liam thought he saw the woman's cheeks start to tint red.

She cleared her throat.

"Or, you know, I can come up with something on my own. It's no biggie, I can—"

Liam cut her off.

"I'll be there. Don't worry."

She cut eye contact with him and cleared her throat again. If he hadn't been looking at her so intently, he wouldn't have noticed her flinch. For a second, he thought it was because of their conversation. Then he really took a good look at her.

She was tired. More pale than usual. Even standing still there was an uncomfortable slant to her.

"Something's wrong with you. What is it?" Liam nodded toward her. "You're hurting somewhere. Where? Don't lie. I can tell."

Blake motioned to her head. Bruce's finger, still wrapped around hers, went with it.

"My head," she said. "We were actually at the store for some sinus meds and ran into Price on his way home. Then I became impulsive and decided to show up here. Price, quite easily I might add, gave up your address with no questions asked. You might want to have a chat with him about that."

Liam had no doubt that the man had a soft spot for Blake, and if it had been just anybody, the information wouldn't have come out.

"Which, by the way, I'm going to go ahead and grab and

take home now," Blake added. "Since I have officially intruded and we've officially come up with a plan, it's time to go home and see if I can't attempt some kind of supper."

The smile looked as tired as she sounded. It was almost the same expression she'd been wearing while sitting in the sheriff's office after Ray and Chase had gone after her.

The McClennan cousins and the same questions came to mind again.

Had they been going after him and gotten her instead? Or had they gone after her trying to shake him?

Coincidence?

Accident?

A poorly laid out plan?

A feeling of protectiveness pushed through him so fast that he didn't have time to think about his words until they were already out there between them.

"I can cook."

HOURS LATER AND all Blake could think was that life sure was a blur.

Next to her in bed was none other than the sheriff of Seven Roads. If she had been a shier woman, she wouldn't have pointed out the oddness. Instead, she snorted and said exactly what was on her mind.

"Had you asked me who would be the first man to share my bed since coming back to Seven Roads, I don't think its sheriff would even be in the top ten of my guesses."

Blake was wearing an oversized baseball T-shirt that read Kelby Creek Fighters and a pair of extremely unattractive flannel sleep shorts. Her wet hair was sloppy in its short braid, and she knew from a hesitant glance in the mirror before getting into bed that her face was pale and flushed all at once.

Her sinus issue had revealed itself to be more of a cold. Before that realization, though, Liam had insisted on following them home to cook. She had started running a fever before Liam had even started making dinner. It had given her enough time to switch to the right medicine and to also let Lola know how *normal* this was. Liam was there as an investigative partner. An acquaintance that had been in the trenches with her during their field escapade.

A friend?

Blake wasn't sure why she couldn't bring herself to label the man as that.

After all, would she let someone less than that into her home? Into her bed?

She glanced over at the man in question. He was sitting next to her with a children's pink plastic desk between them. On its top was an empty bowl of chicken noodle soup.

If he was offended by her joke, he didn't show it. Instead, he actually lobbed one back.

"Funny, I thought this was exactly how I was going to spend my first bedroom experience with the opposite sex after my divorce."

Blake let her mouth hang open for a second. He laughed after seeing her expression.

"What? You didn't expect the quiet guy to make a divorce joke?"

Blake couldn't help herself.

"No," she admitted. "I'm still getting used to hearing you say more than one or two words at a time, and now you're getting personal? Maybe the cold meds are making me hallucinate."

Liam rolled his eyes, but there was a good-naturedness to it. He pointed to the covers that had shifted off her when reaching for the TV remote. Wordlessly, Blake pulled it back up and over her lap. Surprisingly, or maybe not, Liam had been quick to take on a mothering roll once he realized she was sick. He'd been fussing after her worse than Lola.

"Stay warm and I'll talk your head off."

Blake wasn't a woman who liked taking any kind of orders but, as Lola had stated during their earlier, very quiet conversation. "If this good-looking man is here to worry about you and cook for you, don't spit in the face of *that* blessing."

So Blake listened to him. When he told her to shower, eat, stay warm, and now when he was on her again about the blanket she kept throwing off.

"Fine," she said. "But give me some backstory on you. And make it something good that would make the rumor mill go wild if they heard it instead of me. Tell me about your life before Seven Roads."

Liam settled back on the headboard, crossed his arms over his chest and stretched his long legs out. There was something slightly endearing about seeing that he wore socks with patterns on them. The pair he had on had little golf flags across them.

"You're not the first person to get a little grouchy with me when I'm telling you what to do when you're sick," he started, humor in his voice. "My unit used to call me the Mother Hen."

"Mother Hen?"

Blake felt the movement of his nod.

"I had a tendency to take care of everyone when they were sick. Even when they didn't want it. I 'made a fuss,' but instead of being a pretty woman, I was treating grown men like little kids." He chuckled. "They were equally grateful and annoyed. Hence the Mother Hen nickname."

Blake heard the pretty comment but latched onto the overall point he'd made.

"Oh, so this little production isn't rare, huh?" She motioned to the empty bowl between them on the desk. "And here I thought the sheriff was giving me special treatment."

Liam played ball with the joke with startling speed.

"The food is the standard package, but the served-in-bed portion is definitely on the secret menu. Morning service has to be ordered separately."

The heat that ran up Blake's neck was fast. It pooled in her cheeks. She was glad, at least, that she could blame the flush on her fever.

"You might not talk a lot, but you sure know what to say when you do," she returned. "That sweet-talking must get all the ladies."

At this, Liam didn't laugh. Blake peeked over at him, worried she had offended him somehow. He was staring right at her. There was a tilt to his head. Almost like a curiosity.

"I don't think I've sweet-talked anyone since the beginning of my marriage. And even then, it wasn't like this."

Blake felt like a parrot the more she spoke with Liam.

"Like this?"

The world went slow for a bit. Liam kept her gaze, then it started searching. She knew he went from her eyes to her lips then to her brow. After that, she lost track. He was tracing her, maybe looking for something? But what?

He opened his mouth—to answer her, right?—but the next sound that came out was from the bedroom door.

"Excuse me."

Blake nearly jumped. Lola was standing in the doorway, all apologetic with her smile. The little girl behind her leg was peeking out, all shy.

"I hate to interrupt, but Clem wants you," the older woman said. She looked at Liam. "Our Blake here started a dangerous trend. When this one doesn't want to sleep, the two of them watch TV in bed for a bit. We call it wind-down time."

Blake was immediately defensive.

"Hey, not all of us can sleep like logs, like you and Bruce," she said. "I personally think it's smart of me and Clem to partner up on a different path sometimes. Isn't that right, Clem?"

She might be a quiet four, but Clem was always vocal about their occasional late-night TV time.

"Yeah!" she exclaimed. Her hair bounced along with her little hop of excitement. After that she was nothing but speed. Liam barely had enough time to move the desk from the middle of the bed as Clem rocketed herself up and into space in the middle of them.

Lola's smile fell. Concern, fast and deep, lined her frown.

"I can come back and get her in a little bit," she offered.

Blake shook her head.

"You can head to bed. I've got her."

Lola was silent a moment. Clem didn't hesitate, becoming a drill and burrowing under the blanket.

"Are you sure?" Lola added.

"I'm sure. I already feel way better thanks to the meds and food." Blake thumbed over at the sheriff. "Worst case, Mother Hen here can give me a hand if I need it."

Liam was fast.

"Don't worry," he said. "I'll make sure they're good."

Lola didn't fight the offer. During the last week, she had continued to talk about his heroics in the field and, now that he had cooked for them and had clearly been accepted by Clem? Blake had a feeling she'd be singing Liam's praises for a good while. Lola told him thank you and wished them a good-night before leaving.

Blake waited a few seconds before whispering to the man at her side.

"You don't have to stick around," Blake tried. "We're just going to watch some TV."

"I don't mind sticking around a little longer." He notably paused. "Unless you want some space."

Blake didn't.

Not from him.

An acquaintance my tushy, she couldn't help but think.

But instead she said, "You can stay."

Liam took the remote off the nightstand next to him. He said only one word next, but it was enough to make the heat in her cheeks grow warmer again.

"Good."

Chapter Twelve

His hip was hurting, but it wasn't because of his old injury.

Liam opened his eyes.

The bed was different. Too big, too soft. He smelled lavender. He felt warm. Light moved across the room.

It was the TV, still on but muted. A cartoon dancing across the screen.

Liam hadn't been sleeping all that much during the last week. He'd be the first to admit that. However, he hadn't realized how tired he'd actually been. He couldn't deny it now though. One second he'd been talking to Blake about their show, and the next?

Liam realized why his hip felt different.

Clem was pressed against his side, wrapped tightly in her blanket and fast asleep. Just as he had been moments before.

He had fallen asleep slightly sitting up.

At Blake's house.

In her bed.

And she wasn't there next to him anymore.

The spot on the other side of Clem was empty. Adrenaline surged as worry took over all his senses.

That surge turned into an all-out flood when he realized he'd not simply woken up on his own. Movement at the side of the bed came at him quick.

Liam reached one arm out above Clem and the other at the person in motion. His hand wrapped around the person's forearm.

It didn't stop that person from moving though. Instead, they brought their face merely inches from his.

"Keep quiet."

The only light in the room was coming from the TV, but it was more than enough to see the green eyes of Blake Bennet. It was easier to see the worry in them. In her. She was still in the shorts and T-shirt she'd worn to bed. Her hair was down and wild. Her skin was warm and slightly slick with sweat.

She lowered herself even closer to him. She angled her chin so her lips were almost against his ear.

"There're two men outside," she whispered. "One has a gun. I can't tell about the other."

That did it.

Liam let go of Blake and eased himself off the bed as she backed up.

"What are they doing?" He kept his voice low and palmed his cell phone off the nightstand. He internally cursed every decision he had made up until now that meant he didn't have his service weapon on him. It was shut away tight in his truck's lockbox. He hadn't intended to stay long at Blake's, certainly not fall asleep there.

Thankfully, Blake had an answer to that problem. She took that wrist and pulled him along to the closet. It was a small walk-in but big enough to hold a safe. She flipped on the light and went right to it.

"I got up for a glass of water and noticed them at the side yard. They were standing in the tree line," she hurried to say. "I can't tell who they are, but it feels like they're waiting. There's no car outside either, so I don't know where they came from. Take this and go look for yourself."

There was only one gun inside. It was a pistol. She handed it to him. Liam grabbed the ammo that had been kept separately. He assembled the weapon.

"You can see them if you look outside the kitchen window."

Liam wasn't slow when speed was needed. He made it to the kitchen by the grace of memory and a few motion sensor nightlights plugged into outlets turning on along the way. The light over the stove was at his side. He could see the men clearly from the window.

Just as Blake described, there were two of them standing at the edge of the yard, the tree line just behind them. They were dressed casually, shirts and jeans, and tennis shoes. One had a dark hat on, the other a gun in the hand hanging at his side. They were too far away for Liam to make out their faces, but even if he had, there was no person in the world who had a reason to be at Blake's home in the late hours of the night, armed with a gun at that.

Liam did some quick mental math. Instead of calling the sheriff's department, he called someone closer.

It was just after two in the morning, but Price answered on the third ring.

Liam didn't waste a second. He forwent any kind of greeting and dove right in.

"I'm at Blake's house and there are two men standing outside. One is armed, I can't tell about the other. We put my truck in the garage earlier so the neighbors wouldn't see. Lola's car is in there too. Blake's is in the driveway. Me, Blake, Lola, and the kids are in here. We have only one gun between us."

After the first statement, the sound of movement had come through from the other side of the call.

"Did you call dispatch yet?" Price asked. Based on the noise Liam assumed he was dressing.

"No. You're closer and I'm thinking we might need help sooner rather than—"

The two men outside turned in tandem toward the trees. Liam watched as a third person stepped out into the open. There was a gun at his hip.

"A third guy just showed up. He has a gun." One of the original two men pointed toward the house. Liam's gut was all-out growling. "Can you call the department on another phone? I want to stay on the line with you."

Price wasn't playing around. His usual casual tone had been hardened into absolute focus.

"I'll use Winnie's. I'm putting you in my pocket on speaker."

The sound of movement let Liam know the man was doing just that. He too followed suit. Liam slid his cell phone into his breast pocket. He didn't want to break the line of sight he had on the three men, but their situation had just changed drastically.

Who were they?

Why were they here?

Their body language wasn't aggressive. It was like they were waiting for something. Or someone.

Blake was on the same wavelength.

"What are they waiting for?" she whispered.

No sooner had the question came out, than an answer followed.

It wasn't at all what they wanted.

A sound echoed from the back of the house. Metal clinking. Cracking? Had they been asleep, it might not have woken them, but now it was like a gunshot in the night.

Blake's hand slid around his forearm.

"That's the back door," she breathed out. "Someone's trying to come in."

Those words would be the last before the chaos of the next several minutes, but before his legs got ahead of him, Liam glanced back through the kitchen window. The men were no longer standing around chatting. All three were looking at the house now.

Liam realized it then.

They weren't waiting to cause trouble. They were waiting for someone else to start it.

PRESSURE MADE DIAMONDS.

Blake didn't talk about or even think about her mother all that often, but her telling Blake this while growing up had firmly stuck into place. If anything was hard or tiring or brought on waves of stress, it was a necessary part of life. In fact, it was almost a good luck of sorts. Without pressure, there would be no diamonds after all.

That had been a soothing saying for Blake as a kid because it had made the most sense. It wasn't a promise of a stress-free life or a guarantee that life would always go the way you wanted it to. It was practical. It was an if-and-when situation. Not a what-if situation.

When life became hard, endure.

Not *if* life became hard.

That's how you became a diamond.

That saying, however, lost some of its shine when their mother left the family behind. Apparently, Blake's mom could be a diamond. Just not with them.

Years and years had passed since the Bennet matriarch had gone her own way, and yet Blake had found that out of everything she learned—good and bad—from her mother, this sentiment was the loudest. The second the back door started breaking, Blake heard her mother's words as if she were standing next to her.

"Pressure makes diamonds, Blakey. All you have to do is endure the squirmy parts first."

There were four people in the house who absolutely couldn't get hurt.

Bruce, Clem, Lola and Liam.

But one of those took the lead quick. It made Blake's heart skip a little beat.

"Get the kids," Liam said, words and movements hurrying. "We don't know how many are coming in. Hide until backup gets here."

He was already moving, gun raised and ready. For a split second Blake was torn. She wasn't used to taking the back seat in situations like this. She was the one who ran in, gun raised and ready to take on the trouble. Then again, she wasn't in her old life. She was in charge of protecting two little ones. From the known and unknown.

And she had no idea how many armed men were coming.

Endure the squirmy parts first, she thought.

Then all thoughts went on autopilot.

Liam outstepped her, pinpoint focus on the back of the house and the continued sound of someone trying to get the door open. He was a wall of strength and grit. Blake wouldn't have known that ten minutes prior, he was fast asleep with a four-year-old had she not seen it herself.

He didn't even have shoes on at the moment.

Yet somehow that made him more intimidating. A man in his home, ready to defend it.

Blake's gaze left him as she went to the bedroom with the most vulnerable Bennet first.

The hallway had four rooms branching off from it before it forked to the right for the guest bathroom and laundry room. The back door was past the last room. Liam disappeared around the corner, the hallway sensor light flashing on low as he went. It was the only source of light as Blake went into the kids' room.

When things became more settled Blake, planned on giving Clem and Bruce their own room but for now, she shut the door behind her, sidestepped Clem's stuffed animals, the bottom of her twin-sized bed, and a cluster of Barbies on the floor until she was at Bruce's crib. His zoo-print onesie had always made Blake's heart feel warm, but seeing it now, the low light from the rocket-shaped lamp in the corner making most of the room visible, and Blake's stomach went to ice.

Why were the men here?

"Endure the squirmy parts." Blake's mother's words sounded in her head again.

Blake went to work.

She started to reach for Bruce but bumped the baby monitor mounted to the crib. It gave her an idea. She kept her voice low, hoped the sound machine would keep her muffled enough to keep the boy asleep, and leaned close to the speaker.

"Lola. Lola." Blake reached into the crib. Bruce didn't startle at her touch. She got straight to the point. "Lola. Men with guns are here. Liam's at the back door. Be quiet and go to my room."

It was dramatic but urgent. Lola was a light sleeper, so hopefully that would get her going.

Bruce, thankfully, wasn't as easy to wake. Blake had him against her with minimal noise coming from him. She knew that wouldn't last long the more she moved.

Blake walked past the Barbie pile and opened the door as slowly as she could. Movement opposite her almost pulled out a yell in reflex. The same must have been true for Lola.

Her eyes were wide as she finished opening her bedroom door all the way.

Bless the woman's speed.

She was still clutching the receiving end of the baby monitor, but she understood her assignment.

Blake nodded toward the primary bedroom to her right.

A heavy thud sounded from her left.

There was no time to investigate.

Lola was quick and quiet as they went to the bedroom at the opposite end of the hallway. As soon as they cleared the doorway, she had the door shut and locked.

"The bathroom," Blake whispered. Another locked door between them and the intruder would make her feel better. Plus the room only had one window, and it didn't open.

Sounds from the hallway became louder. If there had been an element of surprise on Liam's behalf, it was undoubtedly gone. Neither woman commented on the escalation. They were focused. Lola took Bruce, and Blake scooped up Clem. As soon as all four were in the bathroom, Blake started moving. She took the blanket she had grabbed from the bed and threw it in the garden tub. Clem went in next. She started to stir. Lola put a hand on her stomach and started patting, Bruce was still asleep against her shoulder. The motion-sensor light next to the vanity cast shadows over Lola's face. She was terrified.

Blake hated it.

That didn't mean she wasn't going to give out the facts.

"There were three men outside near the trees," she whispered. "Liam called in backup, but then someone started coming in the back door. At least two of the three outside were armed."

Lola had, as far as Blake knew, never been in a violent situation like this. She didn't own a gun, she had never been in a fight, and the most chaos she had endured had to do with the children she was currently guarding.

But now, she was a diamond.

Her voice was even as she asked a practical question.

"Do we have guns?"

Blake shook her head.

"Liam has the only one in the house."

Fate was interesting.

No sooner than she answered, the house was rocked by a sound that Blake had hoped never to hear.

A gunshot.

After that, no one stayed quiet.

Chapter Thirteen

Ray McClennan hadn't expected Liam to be waiting for him inside the house. That much was evident when Liam had slid behind him, gun raised and pressed it to the small of his back.

"Don't move." Liam's voice had been deathly quiet, but he knew Ray heard him loud and clear.

It's just that the man didn't care to listen.

He spun around while throwing himself off-balance on purpose. It was a wild move that might have had him dodging a bullet had Liam intended on shooting the man on the spot. There were two reasons why he didn't want to use a gun if he could help it.

One, he didn't know exactly where the Bennet family was inside the house, and no matter how great his aim was or how close he was with his target, there was always the possibility that something could go wrong. He didn't want to chance an accident with Blake, Lola, or the kids close by.

Two, and this was just as strong as a point as the first, Liam didn't want the men outside to know that their presence was needed. He wanted them to keep standing next to the trees while they thought Ray had everything handled.

A shot going off in the night surely would do the opposite.

So Liam kept his finger away from the trigger and instead dealt with Ray with the length of his arm and elbow.

He used this and his sheer weight as a battering ram. Instead of going forward, however, he smashed into the man's side and threw him into the laundry room's wall.

Something cracked, but Liam wasn't in the position to inspect. He just knew that Ray hadn't been put out of commission. The man swung his elbow out with undeniable panicked strength. Liam was too close and took the hit to the side of his face.

Pain burst along his cheek.

He didn't have time for it either.

Using his gun as a fist, he brought its butt against Ray's shoulder. It was such an odd spot, but the sudden force did wonders. Ray grunted and tried his best to grab the new pain while also trying to dance away from it.

Space bloomed between them, and in that space, Liam was able to see that Ray wasn't one of the men without a weapon.

He had a gun.

The shot was quick but sloppy. It could have been a kill shot, easy, but Ray was still operating like he had been caught off guard. Instead of a direct chest or head shot, pressure pushed into Liam's right arm. Liam lost his grip on the gun.

So he kicked it away from both of them on reflex as Ray lunged forward with his left.

Liam's hand wrapped around Ray's wrist, and he pulled back with all his might. This time he knew the cracking he heard was the man's bone.

Ray howled in pain. More importantly, he dropped his gun to the wood floor.

Liam kept going. He brought Ray's broken wrist and arm with him as he got behind the man put him in a hold. His plan was to use his knee and the hold to put Ray on the floor.

He never could have accounted for what happened next.

A man wearing a rain slicker and a head so bald it shone

with the limited light appeared in the back doorway. He was
built like the letter T, and although he wasn't the same height
as Liam, he wasn't far off either.

He also had a gun that he didn't hesitate to use.

Liam had no room to move once the gunshot split through
the air.

Neither did Ray.

Still pinned against Liam's chest, Ray took the full force
of the shot to the chest, and it pushed both men over, Liam
hitting the floor hard. The air left his lungs. He struggled
to stand and breathe all at once, coughing and trying to pull
Ray out of the way at the same time.

He was left unprotected. Vulnerable. An easy target.

He should have remembered Sheriff Trouble was still in
the house.

Liam watched in bewildered awe as Blake coolly walked
around him and planted herself near his feet. Her arm was
raised. Liam realized a beat too late that Blake had a gun.

And she wasn't waiting for an invitation to use it.

Blake opened fire with a steady hand and even steadier
focus.

Liam collected his breath and awe to not waste the attack. He looped his arm around Ray's waist, then pushed
and pulled him around the corner and into the longer main
hallway that split the house.

The second he was clear, he yelled back as much to Blake.

She let out the third shot and then was a flurry of motion
rounding the corner.

"He ran," she hurried to say. "No hit."

"Are you okay?"

Blake nodded. If Liam had more time, he would have
really taken the situation in, looked at the woman and her
calm, but now everyone outside knew they were needed.

Though, he was hoping the shots had scared them away. Liam was hauling Ray into the first room to their left when Blake slipped the phone out of his pocket.

The light flashed on at the movement. He could see he was still on the call with Price.

"Price, Ray's been shot, maybe dead, and Liam looks like he took a bullet to the arm too," she hurried. "There's a man in a dark red rain jacket, bald, with a gun. I think I scared him off, but he might come back. The other two are unaccounted for."

Liam straightened to stand.

He'd been shot in the arm?

"The kids and Lola are locked in my bathroom," she added. "I'm putting you back in Liam's pocket and hushing until y'all get here."

Blake did exactly as she said. She put the phone in Liam's pocket and set her gun back to ready.

"Can you still fight?" she asked him. Her eyes flashed to his right arm.

That pressure he felt earlier was starting to fill with pain. He guessed Ray's shot hadn't just been a graze.

That wasn't going to stop Liam.

He nodded.

"Take the gun and stand guard in the bedroom. I can handle things out here."

Blake didn't like that.

Her voice was steel.

"I'm not leaving you."

It was such a direct and resolute statement that Liam was momentarily caught off guard. He wanted to combat it in the next, but the sound of footsteps sounded near the back door.

Were they really that brazen to come in despite knowing the people inside were armed?

Then again, hadn't the bald man shot Ray without hesitation?

Was he coming back with help? Were they about to be caught by three men instead of one?

Blake had her hand wrapped around the gun. She positioned her body to have the best shot at whoever came into view.

It wasn't a good angle.

It would leave her exposed if she wanted a good shot.

Liam had an idea.

He took his phone out and as low as he possibly could, he whispered out a command.

"Price, make noise."

The second the words left his mouth, Liam tossed his phone across the hallway and into the bedroom opposite them. There was a faint light in the room, and because of it, he saw the phone hit something that looked like a pillow on the ground.

The soft thud was still enough to alert whoever had come inside.

Then Price started making noise.

Liam placed his hand on Blake's shoulder. He moved her soundlessly back a few steps. Then his hand dropped to her waist. He adjusted her stance until she was squarely looking into the other room. She didn't fight him.

The footsteps were in the hallway next to both doors.

Price continued making noise on the other end of the phone. There must have been a sound machine going in that room. It made Price sound even more natural, as if there were people trying to talk in hushed, hurried voices.

Liam hoped it would be enough to draw whoever was in the hallway that way first.

He slid his hand back up to Blake's shoulder and kept it there.

She didn't as so much as breathe.

That's how they were standing when the first man came into view. He wore a baseball cap and jeans. There was no gun in his hand but a slight tremor in the way he slowly moved. Liam squeezed Blake's shoulder lightly. She continued to be still.

Which was a feat in itself considering the baseball-capped man made a stunning move.

Instead of walking into the room opposite them, he started to walk backward into theirs.

Liam put pressure on Blake's shoulder with his index and middle fingers. Two quick prods. The man slowly backing up into their space was also using his hands to wordlessly signal. He motioned forward to the room where Price was still doing whatever it was to draw any and all attention.

It seemed the man was going to let his friend do the work of fighting while he backed himself away into a safer space.

Which meant that maybe he really wasn't armed.

And meant that his friend probably was.

Liam released his hold on Blake and took a step forward. Blake didn't move a muscle. He wished he could tell her his plan, but there was no time.

They were outnumbered, and he was hurt.

If they didn't execute the next part of his new plan flawlessly, they could lose their lives. Or, worse, the family hiding in the house could.

But they were also out of any other good options.

So Liam did something he hadn't done since he was in the Marines.

He decided to trust another soul explicitly, no room for hesitation or second thought.

Just pure, unbridled trust.

Then, and only then, did Liam make his move.

THE MAN SEEMED to have no idea he wasn't alone. He had even less of an inkling that the wall of strength that was Liam was waiting behind him. Had he walked back even one more step, he would have collided with him. Instead, he stopped within the relative darkness, staring straight ahead.

He was waiting for his friend and his gun to make the first move.

Too bad for them that Blake and Liam had their own plan.

One that happened in a flash.

A new figure entered the space in front of the man. All Blake could see over his shoulder was that it wasn't the man in the rain jacket. The way he held himself, though, she was almost certain he had a gun in hand.

Liam must have seen it too.

Without a word, he sprung into action and Blake was ready for it.

Liam wrapped his arm and hand around the man in the hat's mouth and torso and pulled them both down and out of the way. The other man about to move into the nursery heard the commotion.

But it was too late.

Now Blake had a perfect line of sight.

There was no room for errors.

She shot her mark with a perfect score.

The man yowled in pain and crumpled.

Then it was a dance between Blake and Liam.

He left the man in the baseball hat on the floor and took two quick steps to the man she'd just sent to the hardwood. Blake didn't watch what he did next but instead switched her attention to the man next to her.

"Don't move," she ground out, gun aimed down at him. "Understand?"

It probably helped matters that Ray's unmoving body was next to him.

She saw his head move in what she assumed was agreement.

Liam took his own unknown man and pulled him into the nursery all the way, keeping himself out of the open hallway.

Blake saw the gun in his hand. The man he had by the back of the shirt was still yowling and thrashing around. It didn't shake Liam one bit.

He met her eye. Shadows danced across his face, but Blake could still see the absolute strength in him.

Now if the bald man appeared, they could outnumber him.

Blake strained to listen for more footsteps. It wasn't easy. The man she had shot in the leg was still wailing. The man on the ground next to her and Ray, however, was obedient in his silence.

Liam looked like he was about to deal with his captive, but another sound broke through the night around them.

Sirens.

And not just one.

Blake didn't dare loosen her defense.

She did, however, let out a small exhale.

Backup had finally arrived.

Chapter Fourteen

Blake slapped her hand down on the table with force. She curled her fingers and dragged her nails against the top until she was making a fist.

"That's Mater Calhoun," she said through gritted teeth. The cell phone next to her showed the image of the smiling man in work clothes. The same man whom she had shot in the leg in her home earlier.

Liam settled into the chair next to her.

"Unfortunate name," he observed. He was mindful of the sling on his arm.

Like several hours before, Price was with them again. This time, though, he was in person, sitting opposite them. It was now morning, but the McCoy County Sheriff's Department paid no mind to the change. The meeting room they were in had one window, and its blinds were drawn tight.

Price shook his head in what seemed to be equal parts anger and disbelief.

That feeling was amplified in Blake.

He could see her fist tightening still. Liam reached out and gently tapped that fist twice.

Blake's gaze flew to him. She silently released her own hold.

"I know of the family but not Mater specifically," Liam

admitted, hand back on his phone. "Other than the obvious reasons why we should be upset, why are you two *this* upset?"

Price was in a full snit, but he acquiesced to Blake for her answer. It almost felt like a hierarchy move, like Blake had seniority, and it was his job to let her take the lead. A part of Liam couldn't blame him for the instinct. Despite being on cold medicine, forced to violence in her own home, and then dealing with the aftermath of getting her scared family together and settled in the sheriff department's break room, she still was a pillar.

Liam didn't know if it made him proud or worried. Or both.

She needed to rest; she couldn't yet.

And apparently, some of that had to do with this Mater Calhoun person.

"Mater Calhoun—" Blake's voice was undeniably angry, even the pause she forced herself to take after his name felt weighted. Whatever she had originally been about to say, she looked like she changed her mind about it. Instead, she was steady with her next words. "He's the reason I left Seven Roads all those years ago."

Liam couldn't help but lean a little toward her.

He quirked an eyebrow.

She was quick to wave her hand at the first thought that sprang up at the statement.

"He was only a friend at the time, and, well, even that's generous," she continued. "He lived on the same block my dad did and liked to come over to the house to hang out a lot. Whether it was with me or Beth, he was an easy guy to get along with. Even my dad liked him, which is saying something." She let out a breath. It was hot with anger still. "Then one day Mater came to the house all upset—like re-

ally upset—saying that he needed my dad's help. He'd gone
and messed up at his summer job at the steel mill and gotten
into a fight with a new hire there, and now everyone wanted
a piece of him, including the sheriff's department."

She snorted. There was no humor in it.

"My dad, someone who'd only had daughters but wanted
sons, told Mater to stay hidden at our place until he could
get things sorted. He told me I was in charge of making sure
he was okay. I didn't mind it at first, but then, well, then I
found out what he did."

Price cut in with a sharper edge than Liam had expected
of him.

"The trouble he'd gotten into was because he beat that
guy so badly that he ended up losing an eye," he said. "And
the man didn't even start the fight. He only swung back in
defense, and even then, he looked like he was pawing at
pillows."

"The security footage of the fight was spread around
pretty decent before Dad could even make it to his lawyer's
office," Blake tagged back in. "I tried talking to Mater about
it, but he just got more and more tight-lipped. But you could
tell he was in the wrong and he knew it. Then he'd come to
the only place in town where someone would fight for him."

Blake looked like she was about to say one thing again
but, instead, switched to something else.

"Then Sheriff Dean showed up on our doorstep," she said.
"He knew my dad saw Mater as a surrogate son and came at
me with the same feeling. He gave me a speech about doing
the right thing, about people who did the wrong thing, and
he really dug deep into the idea that one bad choice doesn't
necessarily mean a life filled with them. But it didn't matter what he said, because I already made up my mind. I let

him in the house and let him take Mater, only stalling long enough to put on my shoes."

Blake's expression grew more solemn. She readjusted in her chair before continuing.

"Dad showed up right as Mater was being driven off by a deputy. He was so spitting mad, face all red and running up like he was about to fight the entire sheriff's department." Blake paused again. This time, Liam knew there was a lot that she wanted to say but didn't. "Sheriff Dean didn't budge at anything my dad said, and after that, my dad never forgave me. We got into a yelling match out near the park on the way home from the department and... Well, it was good for everyone that I left town. Mater, even with a lawyer, ended up in prison later. His sentence was ten years, last I heard."

Blake looked to Price.

He nodded confirmation.

"He got out early for good behavior but stayed out of Seven Roads until a few years ago," he said. "He's been living in the duplex out on Grantham Street. He married a woman he met after he got out. Forget her name, but would you believe where she works? Steel mill. Same place that caused him all the grief. That's probably why he's been doing so many odd jobs through the years, trying to make enough to get her to leave the place."

"And tonight he was with Ray," Liam finally said.

"And tonight he was with Ray," Blake repeated.

Price shook his head.

"I'm guessing that Ray really could be targeting you, Sheriff," he said. "First they go after your dinner companion in the field and now this? Ray might've hired Mater to help, and Mater's been hard up on cash, so he said yes to it. That's best I can guess as to why Mater would get involved. As far as I know, Mater doesn't have a connection to Missy, her father, or her case. I wish we could just ask Ray though. At least get him to tell us who Rain Slicker Guy and Baseball Cap Guy are."

Liam had been able to leave the hospital within an hour of the ambulance dropping their party off. The bullet wound in his arm had been only a little more severe than a graze. He'd needed stitches, sure, but he could manage just fine now. Ray, on the other hand, was in much worse shape and fighting to stay alive. The bald man had done a serious number on him.

Which was one more reason why Liam felt the urgency to find him, the savage one who had managed to run off earlier. The other man with the baseball cap who hadn't even attempted to understand his surroundings, had buttoned up his mouth with speed. No one had recognized him, but Detective Williams would make quick work of him, Liam was sure.

Mater wasn't one to help with this problem either. He was in the hospital post-surgery for his gunshot to the leg. Despite his yelling, he wouldn't say much of anything with or without a lawyer.

"I still don't understand why they're coming after you," Price said after a moment, turning his gaze to Liam. "I mean I kind of understood misplaced anger coming in from his dad because you're looking into Missy's death, but grabbing three other guys and busting into a family home just to— what? Scare you? Hurt you? I don't get it." Price dragged his hand down his face. "Darius is talking to Chase McClennan in a few hours, so maybe we can get some kind of answer there if Darius can't grab anything from Baseball Cap Guy."

Chase McClennan's alibi had been solid. He definitely wasn't at Blake's home that night. Still, that didn't mean he didn't know the men who had been.

Liam looked sidelong at Blake.

He was angry for many reasons, but the grief that Blake

had been put through topped the list. Seeing her worry over the kids and Lola had made him exponentially more so, considering he was the reason they had been traumatized in the first place.

He should have kept his distance from the woman.

That's why he had kept so quiet during the last week. That's why he had asked to put the truck in the garage while he was at her home—to sidestep gossip, sure, but to also keep his associations with her as limited as possible in the public's eye.

He should have actually kept his distance instead, not offer himself up the second she came around.

Now she was going through trouble again because of him.

Liam could feel the anger in his chest boil again. It hadn't left since the night before.

If he hadn't been around, they would be enjoying their morning together in peace, not sitting in the department scared.

"But they didn't know you were there."

Liam's eyes widened as Blake spoke. For a split second he wondered if he had spoken his last thought aloud.

"What?" he asked.

Blake was staring at the fist she had made earlier. She brought her gaze slowly up to Liam's before repeating herself.

"They didn't know you were there."

The men stopped. Liam tilted his head a little, thoughtful.

"We didn't plan on you coming to my house last night," she explained. "Your truck was locked up in the garage and out of sight, and then we all fell asleep. You stayed late on accident. If *we* didn't even know you were going to be there, then how would they?"

"They could have followed you?" Price said.

"But why did they seem so surprised when Liam started

fighting?" she ventured. "Surely they would have expected him to do so. Instead, Ray and Mater waited before coming in. They—"

"They didn't plan on me," Liam interrupted. "Ray seemed genuinely surprised when I appeared. I thought maybe because it was late and they expected us to be asleep, but the sight of me made him hesitate."

Blake nodded, unclenched her fist and used her index finger to tap out another point on the tabletop.

"They followed me last week. Maybe they really had no idea you were driving behind me. You weren't ever in their plan."

Price was shaking his head.

"So—what?—you're saying that they came just to break in? To what? To rob you when they knew you and the kids would be home? There's got to be easier places to get a nicer score, no offense."

She shook her head.

"Even if I had a house full of valuables, why would you bring *that* much manpower? Why bring *four* men, armed, to a home when everyone's supposed to be sleeping?" She met Liam's eye again. "And why, even if that's your plan to break in and steal, do you send only one out when you know resistance is probably going to happen?"

Liam was sure of it now.

"They had no idea I was there," he agreed. "They expected only you to be a threat."

Blake tapped her finger against the table again.

"Which brings us to another question we might have an answer to," she said. "Why not wait until we weren't home? We have a set routine taking the kids to daycare and doing errands when none of us would be home. When there wouldn't even be a chance of resistance. But instead, it's like they came prepared for battle…a battle they didn't think you would be there for."

Price's eyebrow rose.

"What are you thinking?" Price said.

But Liam had already followed her thought process.

He wasn't a fan of where it led.

"They came for you."

APART FROM SOME THEORIES, they didn't have a strand of evidence to make sense of the men or their actions. Sitting there talking about it wasn't helping either. Try as she might to appear the epitome of composure, Blake was finally starting to openly struggle.

Not only had she missed sleep and gone through a traumatic experience in which she'd had to shoot someone, there was the simple and annoying fact that she had a cold tugging at her. Her head hurt, her nose was starting to stuff up again, and although she didn't feel as if a fever was hanging around, there were a few body aches that were nagging her.

When Liam said it was time for her to go, however, she was split between agreement and a stubborn need to stay. She pushed; he didn't budge. He told her no once more to her suggesting she go in to talk to Mater or the man who'd worn the baseball cap with absolute resolution.

"Running yourself ragged isn't going to help anyone," he said, standing tall in front of her in his office. "Not you, your family, or solving whatever is going on here. So let's go."

Even though the sheriff had been a lot more social with her in the last twenty-four hours or so, Blake found that it was her turn to hesitate at the sight of him. It wasn't the first time she had wondered how she and her family would have fared if he hadn't been there to help. She eyed his bandaged bicep and the sling keeping his arm steady.

Her mind wandered to perhaps the real reason she wasn't ready to leave.

If she hadn't already been preoccupied, she would have avoided his next movement.

Liam stroked a warm thumb down between her eyebrows, smoothing out the crinkle there.

"Go ahead and tell me what you're thinking," he said. "That way I can join the conversation."

The touch might have unsettled her before, but now she sighed as it withdrew.

"Let's say that I really am a target. Is it because of you? Because of me? Because of Missy's case? Or what if it's belated revenge from me turning on Mater back when we were young with an added bonus of Ray helping?"

"There's no way we can know yet," Liam pointed out.

"Exactly. Which means, how can we know if Rain Slicker Guy isn't out there waiting to try again? Whether it's against me or you." She put her hand to her chest. "I'm good with me being in a bull's-eye, but what about the kids? Lola? Won't me being with them put them in danger again?"

Liam did something so unexpected, all Blake could do was stare.

He laughed.

"What did you think I was about to do?" he asked when done. "Send you off alone?"

Blake didn't respond. That's exactly what she thought.

He shook his head. His voice thrummed low and strong as he explained.

"Until we have this whole thing figured out and settled, I'm not leaving your side. Sorry to say, you're stuck with me now, Sheriff Trouble. And that's that."

Chapter Fifteen

Once that decision was made, Blake and Liam didn't speak much.

It was understandable, they both were moving parts that needed to be moved. Liam saw to the department, assigned jobs and made phone calls while doing both. Blake wasn't connected to his movements but was always near. She had the kids, her and Lola packed in a flash. In the next, she had them unpacked at the only house in Seven Roads that could be considered a secret.

At least, according to Price.

"A lot of people don't know this, but I once tried my hand at flipping houses a few years before you showed up," he explained once Liam and him had inspected every inch before ushering the Bennet clan inside. "And by 'tried my hand,' I mean I've been renovating my aunt's house for a long time… with a slow hand and thin patience."

He pointed to the field behind the two-story home and then brought it around to the two houses on either side, though with a lot of space between all three.

"This backs up to the Becker Farm's western pasture and no one's home in any of these. They've been that way for ages though. One's an inheritance to a city dweller who hasn't set foot in town in years, and the other has another lazy renovator who hasn't done much over the years."

"And no one knows you own this place and you're letting us all stay here." Liam wanted to make sure.

Price nodded.

"Despite popular belief, there *are* some places in town that even gossip gets bored of. No one comes out here anymore. There's no point in it." He clapped Liam on the back and smiled. "That said, I'm not a man who just leaves an empty house sitting alone. This baby has a security system and cameras around the outside and the inside of the front and back door. If anyone comes by unannounced, you'll know it quicker than a second sneeze."

Price didn't add onto the fact that, unlike last night, this time Liam was also prepared. His service weapon, along with a bag he'd packed quickly, had definitely come along with them.

"Thanks for this," Liam said once they had done another recap of what needed to be done next. "I know as sheriff I probably should be hanging around the department during a time like this but…"

He didn't finish his sentence. He didn't have to for Price to understand. Or for him to respond about the woman on his mind.

"Sheriff Trouble and her family have been through a lot already. If you can help ease some of their burden, I would think less of you if you didn't try." Price smiled. That smile changed a little in the next moment. "Plus, from what I know of her, Blake doesn't often let people into her life so easy, never mind letting them help her. Other than Lola, I can't think of a single person she'd let get as close as you've gotten to her and the kids. It'd be a waste if you didn't use that to help her out."

Liam couldn't deny that hearing those words meant a little more than they maybe should have. It felt like only yesterday that he had handed Blake his shirt, and yet at the same time, he realized he was as comfortable around her as if she had been in his life for a long while.

Though, his lack of information on her was a quick reminder that that wasn't the case.

A question that had been in the back of Liam's mind came out of his mouth.

"By the way, did anything else happen with Mater Calhoun? Back then, I mean. When he was arrested."

Price's eyebrow went up in question. Liam clarified his meaning.

"Anything else, that is," he said. "When Mater was brought up, you and she just seemed to have a lot of anger directed toward him. A lot more than I thought there would be for the situation. I was wondering if there was part of the story I was missing."

They were standing in front of Price's cruiser, a good distance from the house and the family inside. Still, he lowered his voice a little when he answered.

"It's not so much about what Mater did as what happened after he was arrested." He nodded toward the house. "Blake really undersold the fight she had with her dad. He was so mad at her for letting the sheriff in to take Mater that he kicked her out of the car downtown on the way home from the department. He yelled at her pretty badly on the sidewalk with an audience and everything."

"What was he fighting with *her* for?" Liam couldn't help but feel defensive.

Price sighed.

"Loyalty. And how she didn't know what that word meant. There was more to it—I wasn't there personally—but a few bystanders at the time stepped in to try to calm him down."

"What did Blake do?"

Price shrugged.

"She took as much as she could stand. Then she yelled

right on back about Mater being in the wrong, and, well,
she kept going. They started yelling about her mom leaving
them, and then suddenly she said she was going to do the
same. She kind of dragged the town through it too, calling it
small and noisy and a place she never ever wanted to come
back to." He shrugged. "We've all said some mean stuff in
a fight before but that's where a lot of Seven Roads's locals
get their anti-Blake feelings from. No matter if she meant it
or not, the rumors and gossip were really bad after that. For
her, her dad, and Mater. A month later she was gone. Hon-
estly, I thought she'd never come home again." The deputy let
out a breath. There was some defeat in it. "Though, I guess
she didn't come back for really happy reasons in the end
since her sister passed. Now…now all of this is happening."

They let that sit for a moment.

Then they said their goodbyes.

Liam watched the deputy drive away with some residual
anger still in his chest.

At Mater, at Blake's father, at the men who had invaded
the Bennet home.

When Liam had told the woman that he wasn't leaving her
side, he had meant it. Now, he somehow meant it even more.

Price's house was furnished but only with the basics. Had
it been just the two of them, it probably would have felt cold
and empty, but when Liam finally went back inside, he was
met with a slew of toys, mats and little knickknacks that
came with the territory of children.

Breadcrumbs, he thought while scooping up a little alien
stuffed creature by the door. He hadn't had much time to interact with Bruce and Clem but had noticed the girl clinging
to the stuffed creature earlier that day.

Liam was going to bring the toy to her when he spotted
someone on the couch in the living room.

Blake looked ready to drop, but when she saw Liam, she gave him a little nod.

"Did Price leave?" she asked.

"Mm-hmm," he confirmed. Liam spotted the baby monitor on the coffee table next to her. He could see Bruce and Clem on the display, both asleep on the main bed.

"Lola's on the couch next to them. She's using nap time to catch up on sleep herself." Liam was about to suggest Blake do the same, but a change overtook her expression so quickly that it momentarily made him pause. She took advantage of the space. "I want to use this time to ask you a question. One I haven't actually asked yet."

Liam felt his eyebrow rise.

"What is it?" he asked.

Blake, obviously tired and in need of sleep herself, had a voice that was suddenly as hard as steel.

Those eyes kept his entire attention as she spoke.

"Whether or not I'm being targeted, or you're being targeted, I'm going to focus on the one thing we've had in common the last week or so."

"Missy Clearwater's death?"

She nodded.

"But now I want you to tell me—why do you really think Missy Clearwater was murdered?"

LIAM HAD TO be tired, but he didn't look it. Instead, he somehow managed to exude an energy that sent a surge of steadiness up Blake's spine. He was calm. He was focused.

He was very good-looking.

It had a cold-water-to-the-face kind of effect on her.

The drag of her cold meds and the aching exhaustion that had been pressing down on her since that morning temporarily disappeared.

"I guess keeping you in the dark isn't going to keep you

safe, like I once thought," he said, a slight teasing in his words. It was another small break from the normally quiet man. She leaned into it with a snort.

"Keeping me in the dark just leaves me in the dark, and I'd like at least a flashlight beam in here," she said in return.

Liam nodded to that. He let out a breath and sank onto the couch cushion next to her. Blake angled her body to be able to meet his eye the best she could, given how the man was just as tall sitting as he was standing.

"First off, are you familiar with Doc Ernest?"

"The medical examiner for the county? Yeah, I know her. More from when we were younger though. She's a good egg."

He nodded again.

"That was my impression of her too, despite not having many reasons to interact with her through the years," he said. "So when she called and told me that she thought Missy was already dead before she hit the ground, I had no reason to not believe her."

"Missy was already dead?"

If that was true, that was news to Blake. And apparently not common knowledge that many others had heard. After first meeting Liam, Blake had scoured the internet for news of Missy's death. No sources had mentioned her taking a post-death tumble.

"It became a several-day conversation between us. One that the doc ended up walking back after having another look at the examination. She said she thought she'd become too emotionally invested since she knew Missy and had been wrong with her original report. I would have left it at that, but I'd already found this. That's when the hunch I haven't been able to get free of came in."

The man was wearing some nice snug-fitting jeans but managed to pull a small black case out of his pocket. He opened it to show a flash drive. It looked like it had seen better days. There were initials written in marker on its side.

"M.C.," Blake read aloud. "Missy Clearwater?"

"I assume so," he said. "Considering I found this under the bridge when I was taking pictures there the day after her death."

Blake didn't reach for the flash drive but leaned in a little as if seeing it closer would give her more answers. The movement put her thigh up against his in the process. If he minded the closeness, he didn't say anything.

"That's a weird thing to have on you normally, never mind before your death," she said. "What's on it?"

At this, Liam's expression grew thoughtful.

"One Notepad document," he answered. "It's a code."

"Code? Like as in computer commands that looks like the green font in the Matrix movies?"

He nodded.

"Exactly that. But according to an old computer hacker friend of mine from college, it's only a partial piece of a much longer series of coding. A copied and pasted snippet from something else."

Blake smoothed over the fact that Liam had casually mentioned having an old computer hacker friend for later discussion and posed another question.

"Why was Missy carrying a flash drive with a partial computer code on it? Are you sure it's hers? Though I guess if it wasn't, it would be one heck of a coincidence. Ugh. I wish we could find her laptop. If she had that code, then the rest is probably there."

Liam was watching her. It was the only reason she didn't go on a stream-of-conscious rant with her thought process. Instead, she bottom-lined the answer to her own original question.

"So, it's all suspicious," she said. "A medical examiner

who wavered on her belief that Missy was already dead when she fell and a flash drive with the unknown code on it near her body. That's how you got your gut feeling that something is seriously off."

Liam dipped his chin down a little.

"And now the missing laptop and the McClennan cousins last week and Ray, plus the three men who came to my house last night, a place that they either did or did not know you were inside of."

Was this whole thing about Missy's case? About the code?

That made more sense than everyone coming at her for no reason.

Blake didn't know the answers, but she knew she wanted to help get them.

"I missed my meet-up with Missy's ex-boyfriend Kyle at the coffee shop, so let's reschedule for tomorrow, if we can, and that way, maybe we can figure out at least where Missy's laptop is or why she might have had this flash drive and code."

Liam was still watching her. Which made sense. They were talking after all.

Yet, Blake stopped herself.

Because, well, it didn't exactly feel like they were on the same page anymore. Instead, it felt like Liam had gone to a different metaphorical book altogether.

Then, as if to prove that point, he did something that froze Blake to spot.

His gaze dropped to her lips.

Adrenaline shot through Blake. Her heartbeat started to gallop with its encouragement.

Slowly, like syrup sliding, he reversed his gaze and trailed back up to her eyes.

Heat, not warmth, but heat ignited within her.

It was surprising; it wasn't surprising.

Liam Weaver was perhaps the only person who Blake had

met in the last few years that she had felt this comfortable with. The only man who she had let into her home so easily. The only man who hadn't made her occupation, her personality and her unusual life choices and circumstances feel less than.

He had helped her. She had helped him. He had a problem. She wanted to help. He wanted to help keep her safe. She wanted to help keep him safe too.

He was so very handsome.

And they were so very close right now.

Blake knew she probably could have helped it, but in that moment, she decided her actions were out of her control.

Liam leaned down, closing the distance between them, and Blake was ready to accept anything he gave. Her eyes almost fluttered closed.

But then a noise made them stay wide open.

"I'm hungry."

Blake whirled around to see Clem standing at the foot of the stairs, eyes sleepy but tummy apparently growling.

Normally, that would have given Blake a laugh. Clem was quiet only until she was hungry, then she would chat the entire alphabet until she had food in hand.

However, when Blake saw her, she couldn't stop the first thought that came into her head.

She looks just like Beth.

All at once, Blake remembered why she was in Seven Roads. Just as she remembered why she left.

And why she hadn't come back. Till now.

Guilt and anger and immense sadness gripped her chest tight.

She got off the couch, not looking back at Liam.

It was for the better.

Blake wasn't back in town for her life after all.

Chapter Sixteen

That night, Blake slept. Though not soundly.

She was sharing a bed with Lola, and Lola was moving to every toss and turn. It wasn't until the morning sun started to creep through the slit in the curtains that the older woman finally whispered into the quiet.

"What's hurtin' on you? Your nose, mind, or heart?"

Blake went still, though she opened her eyes wide. There was no use in pretending she had been anything but restless.

"I think I'm finally over the hump with this cold crud I got from the kids," she hedged at first. "Liam gave me the nod of approval after supper, if you don't believe me."

"So, not the nose. Then is it the mind or heart that's got you all jumbling the sheets?"

Blake sighed.

She could lie, but with everything Lola had done for her, there wasn't a good enough reason in the world to tell the woman anything but the truth.

Too bad the truth for her wasn't as easy to answer herself.

"I'm not sure," she admitted. "I keep thinking about how close y'all were to danger. Clem for the second time. I keep thinking about Liam's arm bleeding. I keep thinking about Mater and Ray. Then I'm thinking about Beth. Then I'm thinking about how she trusted her kids to me, and I'm already having to shuttle them off to a safe house with no clear plan on how to make sure they stay safe."

Blake let out another long breath. Even though she was lying down, it felt like she was dragged farther down into the mattress.

"I think the loudest thing in my head is Beth," she added. "She's probably looking down at me, wondering why it's me who's here and not the other way around."

Blake knew she had a lot on her plate that she could have been mentally chewing on, but that thought seemed to have been bothering her the most.

There she had been thinking about kissing the sheriff when she should have been thinking about how to get the kids back to their normal, safe lives.

Beth wouldn't have her kids in danger and thinking about anything else.

She was ashamed even now at the move.

A shame Blake thought Lola would understand.

However, the older woman did something she hadn't expected.

"I'm sorry."

Those two words were enough to get Blake's head to turn on her pillow. Lola was staring up at the ceiling.

"You're sorry?" Blake repeated. "Why? What for?"

There wasn't a thing Lola Bennet ever had to be sorry for, at least not to Blake's knowledge. Still, she sure did sound it in those two words.

She kept staring at the ceiling as she spoke.

"Beth dying was a dang shame, there's no two ways about that," Lola started. "Her leaving behind those two angels in the other room, well that makes her passing hurt even more. Knowing that they won't get to know their mama and knowing she won't get to raise them... It sure does hurt.

But, Blake, she's gone and her going doesn't take away from something I don't guess anyone has talked about yet."

Lola reached out. Her hand wrapped around Blake's over the covers.

"You lost your life too. The moment you learned she passed was the moment your life jumped track. Everything you worked for, your career, your dreams, the life you were building, and the life you had planned…it ended when you knew Beth was gone."

Lola squeezed her hand.

"And, honey, you didn't bat an eye at it. You packed up that life, those dreams, your everything, and you came back to a place you didn't want to, and you stood tall. You didn't have time to prepare, and more importantly, you didn't have time to grieve. And I'm not talking about grieving Beth. I'm talking about grieving you. The life *you* lost."

She sighed.

"I bet you talked to countless people during your time in law enforcement about moving on after tragedy. After the death of loved ones. I bet you spoke about peace and time healing wounds. But I'm starting to think that, maybe, you haven't actually seen that your loss needs some peace too."

Lola squeezed her hand again. Blake didn't dare move.

"Beth is gone," she said. "From now until we go, that won't change. But you? You're here, kiddo. Every choice you make is yours now. Beth can't do a thing, and if you ask me, Beth wouldn't if she could. She'd know as well as I do that while we can tell those children about her and do our best to make sure they never forget her, *you* are going to be the mama who takes them through most of their lives."

She let go of Blake's hand. The sudden lack of warmth startled her. She turned to see Lola had turned to look at her.

"Beth might not agree with every little thing you decide

to do in your life, but don't you forget for a second that she picked you to take care of the most important things in hers. So don't be too hard on yourself. You've done everything just right, even the wrong things. Stop putting your life on hold because you think you have to live Beth's. It isn't fair to you, her or the kids if you stop being Blake." She reached out and put a hand on Blake's cheek. The baby monitor for the kids asleep in the guest bedroom next door cast a glow across Lola's face. Blake saw her smile. "And I'm sorry that no one has said any of this to you yet. To be fair, I would have said it sooner, but, well, I've also never had to raise little ones and— my goodness—they sure make the time fly by."

She rubbed her thumb across Blake's cheek. It pushed the tears running down it away.

Blake hadn't even realized she had started crying.

After a moment, when Lola pulled her hand back, she laughed a little.

"Did I ever tell you what my favorite thing about my father was?" Blake asked. She ignored the slight rasp to her voice.

Lola shook her head.

"No. What?"

Blake smiled.

"The fact that he made you my mom."

Lola paused, caught off guard no doubt by Blake showing such emotion. That shock didn't last long.

"That's funny, because you want to know my favorite thing that man ever did was?" she asked.

"What?"

Lola's smile grew.

"He made you girls."

After that, there wasn't much to say. Blake cried a little more; Lola consoled her with pats and hand squeezes. The sun rose higher outside and the room grew brighter. Eventually, the weight pressing against Blake's chest started to lift.

Then, sometime after that, her thoughts found their way to Liam.

Blake thought it was important that she started to feel even better after that.

Price was going above and beyond his job as a deputy. In fact, he seemed to be going above and beyond that of a friend too. Liam only said the former in a comment at the dining table after lunch.

"I can't order you to stay here," he told the man again. "So if it's not something you have time for…"

Price, who was dressed down in street clothes and had his daughter, Winnie, in the kitchen behind them with Lola, waved the concern away.

"Listen, I wouldn't offer to do this if I wasn't confident in my abilities, the safety of this house and the fact that I think you have a better chance at getting the information we need to potentially put this entire fiasco to bed than me." Price looked down at Liam's lap.

Or, really, Clem.

Since that morning the little girl had been stuck to his side, in his arms and on his lap. It seemed returning her alien stuffed creature had curried unflappable good favor for him. Liam wasn't complaining. He was quick to notice that she was quick to notice things herself. They had made fast work of the two puzzles that Lola had brought along in their toy bag. Even a tablet game about cupcakes had been a breeze for the two of them.

Now she was holding her alien and watching Price speak like she was memorizing every inch of the man and his words.

He smiled at her, but Clem didn't return the gesture. Instead, she leaned her weight back against Liam's chest and just kept staring.

"Tough crowd," Price muttered. There was humor in it though.

Liam snorted, but it was Lola who came in with a comment.

"Don't act like Blake hasn't given you the same look before," she said. "The Bennet women need to scrutinize before they fraternize."

She stopped next to Liam and held out her hand to the girl.

"Though, I will say, Sheriff, you've sure earned the acceptance of the very same women in record time." Price couldn't see the wink that Lola threw him. He cleared his throat as her attention went to Clem. "Now, it's time for Sheriff Weaver and Sheriff Trouble to go get some answers, so why don't us girls and Bruce go watch a movie with Miss Winnie? I heard she brought us *Frozen*, which I'm pretty sure is your—"

Clem was already throwing herself off Liam at the mention of *Frozen*. All three adults laughed as the four-year-old started to sing one of the movie's songs as she ran into the living room.

"That's my cue," Lola said. She started to leave the room but paused as Blake walked in. Liam watched as she lightly tapped the back of Blake's hand before telling her to be safe. "That's to you too, Sheriff. I know Blake here is trouble, but let's keep it to a minimum if we can."

He nodded to her.

"Will do."

"And that's my cue to tell y'all the same," Price said. He stood between them and told them to be safe and to keep him in the loop. He also reiterated his vigilance in keeping the family safe on his end.

Then it was just the two of them.

Liam made sure to keep his gaze firmly locked with hers.

Not on the outfit that looked so good on her, not on the way her small smile made the room feel brighter, and not on the way her lips shone with whatever makeup she had put on for their outing.

Liam had already messed up the day before. One second he had been listening to her excitedly rattle off ways to help him solve their current complicated questions, and the next he'd wanted something so simple all other thoughts had left his mind.

He wanted to kiss her.

That was it.

Liam wanted to kiss Blake in the middle of their chaos. Not out of worry or pity or attraction only.

He had wanted to be closer to her, simple as could be.

It had been such a strong yet singular desire that he had thought about it for a long while later that night when alone on the couch.

No matter what he was feeling, no matter why, he wasn't about to make Blake uncomfortable. Something he had clearly already done by the move. So he had made a resolution to keep things professional as could be.

As normal as could be.

Definitely no thinking about how beautiful she was.

Definitely no staring at her lips.

So he cleared his throat again and returned her small smile.

"Ready to go?" he asked.

Blake nodded.

"Are you ready to keep your cool around a man we both have already agreed we dislike?"

Liam grumbled as he grabbed his keys. He waited until

they were inside his truck and pulling out to answer with words.

"You get this no-good guy talking and I'll keep him going," he said. "But I'm here to let you know that if you had asked me last week if I was going to tag along on a coffee date with Kyle Langdon, I never would have had meeting Missy's ex for a coffee date on my Bingo card."

Blake let out a chuckle.

"If it means we might figure out where that laptop of hers is, you'll just have to learn to endure there, Sheriff."

Liam grumbled again.

"I just don't get a man like that," he said after they made their way back to the main road. He didn't say it, but Liam had been focused on making sure no one was around or following them. He had no doubt Blake was doing the same.

"What do you mean? A man who cheats, or a man who immediately gets with his girlfriend's best friend after they break up?"

"Both," Liam said. "But what I meant was how he's taken Missy's death. No matter how it happened or why it happened, he doesn't seem…like I think he should. I mean, they broke up, and a week later this happened to her. I've been divorced from my ex for years, and I think I'd still be upset if she died."

The thought was true, but Liam felt the need to correct it just a little.

"I mean not because I still have feelings for her like that but just because she's a human I used to spend all my time with." He shook his head. "Unless he's really just a despicable piece of scum, I would have thought he would be more… affected. Even with his new girlfriend."

"Maybe he's hiding it," Blake offered.

Liam shrugged.

"He did, and is doing, a good job of it then. Might have to tell him to try his hand at acting."

She let that thread of thought sit. A small silence stretched between them.

Blake broke it a few blocks before they made it the Twenty-Two Coffee Shop.

"How long were you with your ex?"

The question came out a little strong. Liam glanced sideways at the woman.

Blake was already looking at him. She rolled her eyes.

"I'm only asking because that's the first time you've brought up some gossip that I've already heard. I figured I'd give you a chance to let me hear *your* side of the story since we're already talking about it."

"Ah, the divorce rumors." Liam laughed. "Theo's told me a few he's heard since I came to town. My favorite one was where I didn't talk to her for a month straight, and that's what pushed us to divorce. Is that what you think happened?"

He was genuinely curious.

Blake was quick with her response.

"You talk to me just fine, so I don't think it's that."

A simple answer.

And it was true.

While he was a quiet guy, he was finding that talking was less of an effort and more natural around Blake.

He didn't say that though.

He took a turn to get them to the community parking lot for Main Street. Then he told her a truth he hadn't said out loud in a long time.

"We got married young—high school sweethearts—and still were growing up together when I went into the Marines. Then I started deploying, and the time we actually spent together became less and less." No matter what mood he was in, no matter who he was talking about, when mention of his time in the military came up, the dull pain in his hip pulsed. Liam fought the urge to readjust in his seat. "I was in an accident on my last deployment and had to come home. That time helped us realize that life for both of us had changed while I was away. We weren't the same kids we were in high school. Though we did try to say together. It just turned into the two of us being unhappy all the time. We divorced after eight years. It was the best option for us."

He smiled as he parked the truck.

He meant it.

"We still keep in touch and wish each other happy birthday and catch up occasionally," he added. "She's remarried to a good guy and they have a little boy and another on the way. It isn't what we thought would happen for us when we first married, but we've already agreed we wouldn't change a thing. We're where we are meant to be now."

It was true, all of it. He wouldn't take away his marriage or the divorce. Both led him to Seven Roads and the driver's seat right next to Blake. He couldn't be mad at that now, could he?

He cut the engine, thinking the topic was well and done, and turned to go over their plan one more time for meeting Missy's ex.

It was wholly a shock to, instead, find Blake already in motion.

She closed the space between them in one fluid movement.

Her lips were warm.

Chapter Seventeen

News of their attack had made it around Seven Roads but, apparently, had a few key facts omitted in the retelling. The first was who exactly it was who broke into the house. Sure, word had gotten caught in the rumor mill nets that Ray and Mater had gone to the hospital, but as for the third and fourth unknown men who had attacked, no one spoke of them.

Blake wondered belatedly if that had been due to Liam's constant low-voice talking he had been doing to everyone who had stepped onto the scene that morning. Or maybe it was fear. There hadn't been an outpouring of violence like this in a long while in town. Maybe they didn't want to incur the unknown men's wrath by idly chatting about them.

Either way, it was perhaps the second piece of information that was absent that really surprised Blake.

No one seemed to know that Liam had been with her.

That was apparent in how Corrie greeted them as they walked into the coffee shop. She side-eyed Blake while motioning to a separate table for Liam.

Her face was wholly shocked when he shook his head and declined.

"I'm with her," he said simply.

Corrie's eyes went wide. Blake's nearly did too.

Heat started to whirl in her belly. Damn that baritone.

Though, could she really only blame the octave of his voice for making her have to fight a blush?

Blake didn't need to have a good memory to recall the fact that no more than two minutes ago, she had kissed the sheriff in the front seat of his truck like they were teens parking. She hadn't lingered as long though. As quickly as she had moved to him, as quickly as she had felt the soft strength of him, smelled some kind of spice on him, heard his breath momentarily pause, Blake had ended the kiss.

Then, as if she had reverted right past that confident teen making out in a parked car mindset, she had settled on an awkward resolution.

Pretend it didn't happen while not addressing it at all.

She'd broken the kiss and then coughed.

Then said, "Let's go."

And, to his credit, Liam had.

Now he stood firm at her side until Corrie redirected her open hands to one of the tables against the window. Instead of following her suggestion, however, Blake felt his hand on the small of her back.

"We'll sit over there instead, thanks."

Blake let herself be guided to a table in the corner of the room with a good sightline to all entrances and exits. She would be lying if she said she didn't enjoy Corrie's dumbfounded expression as they walked around her.

There wasn't time to talk, or not talk, about their kiss as Blake settled into a chair. Liam left her to go to the main counter to order, and no sooner had he done that, a man with golden floppy hair and a too-wide smile came into the coffee shop.

Kyle Langdon, Missy Clearwater's ex-boyfriend.

Like she couldn't deny seeing Corrie baffled by Liam

wanting to be next to her, there was no denying that Kyle heard the news about the attack.

He was barely holding it together as he took the seat opposite Blake. He didn't even notice Liam or Corrie at the counter.

Which was good. That way he wouldn't leave before she could start prying.

"Are you okay?" Kyle said. He had those big doe eyes and they suited him nicely. He was handsome and, she'd bet, charming. The stereotypical image of a good old Southern fraternity brother who went to the beach for spring break and wore the same shirt for every football game his team played.

Blake smiled into his concern.

"Bad news travels fast, I see. But I'm good. I just needed a change of scenery, is all."

She motioned to the room around them. Kyle's eyes were glued to hers.

"I bet! I couldn't believe it when I heard, and then you texted me to reschedule? I really couldn't believe something like that happened here in town."

Blake had already suspected that Kyle would hear the news and, with it, would figure out who she was with all the additional town talk through the years. Kyle, however, went in a different direction.

"If I knew you were Beth's sister, I would have been way chattier when we first met."

Blake, who had been at the ready to pepper in questions that would lead to Missy and her life right before her death, stalled. She'd been 100 percent focused on a Missy conversation. Talk of her sister hadn't even been on her radar.

"Beth? You knew my sister?"

The Bennet family had never been a simple one. Their go-to family move was to leave after all. Their mother, Blake,

Beth's husband, and then their dad after Beth's death. Even Beth had found a way to go, though she hadn't intended to. There had been a lot of time between Blake's exit and Beth's, and logically, Blake had known that.

But, sitting across the table from the smiling man, Blake finally understood that space. She had no idea if Kyle Langdon knew her sister. She had no idea if they had been friends. If they had passed each other on the streets every day or went to the same church. If they only knew of each other or if they had gone to a party or two as friends.

And it wasn't just Kyle.

The last time Blake had spoken to Beth about her life and not just updating her about her own, they had been texting. Beth was trying to remember a song but hadn't known enough of the words to search it. So she'd sent a voice message to Blake humming it poorly. Yet Blake had gotten it and answered correctly. Beth had been excited and said thanks.

Remember to eat something yummy was the last text she got back from Beth after.

Then, a month later, Beth was gone.

Blake might have known the song, but she was faced with an awful coldness of realization now.

She had already lost her sister before she had even died.

Kyle, however, didn't have a clue in the world about the emotional turmoil Blake had just found herself in. He nodded to her question with enthusiasm.

"Of course I knew Beth," he said. "I was there when she tore Mr. Grant a new one."

"Tore Mr. Grant a new one?" she repeated.

Kyle nodded deep.

"We couldn't believe it, you know, the factory workers in that section," he said. "I've been at the steel mill since high school and never seen someone even raise their voice at Mr. Grant, and there she was with a red face and so loud."

Blake was stunned.

"What was she yelling about?"

Kyle still hadn't caught on that he had, once again, thrown her for an emotional loop.

He shrugged.

"I couldn't hear the specifics, but I think he turned down one of her suggestions for something to do with the furnaces. But to be fair, he gets a lot of suggestions from safety advisors so—"

"When did this fight happen?" Blake interrupted. Her voice had raised but she couldn't help it. Kyle's eyebrows went higher with it. He looked like he was finally realizing that he had said something that bothered her.

"Uh, she never really came to the steel mill unless she was working, so I guess that was around..." He let his words trail off. His eyes widened. "Oh, man. I'm sorry. I didn't think—"

The chair scraped against the tile as Blake pushed it back and stood. She crossed the room in one fluid movement, only pausing at the counter for one question.

"Is Cassandra in the back?"

Corrie had a coffee cup stopped midair between her and Liam.

She nodded.

"She's on a call—"

Blake kept moving, eyes on the hallway that led to the office.

She heard Liam ask after her, but there was no stopping her.

Blake flung open the manager's office door and closed it right back behind her once inside. Cassandra was indeed on the phone, but Blake took it from her and slammed it down on the cradle to hang up.

Cassandra seemed rightly angry, but Blake spoke over any and all questions and concerns.

"Why didn't you tell me that Beth fought with Mr. Grant before she died?"

Cassandra took the words and spat back a question with just as much heat.

"What the heck do you mean?"

Blake pointed in the direction of the main room behind her.

"Kyle Langdon said he saw Beth yelling at Mr. Grant at the steel mill and Beth only went there twice in the last year. Once to do the inspection on the furnaces and the day she died. How come I didn't hear about the fight? You had to have known!"

She was so angry. So heated. Her hands shook, her heartbeat sped.

Had the fight been the reason Beth had been speeding? Had it distracted her and led to the accident that killed her?

Why hadn't a town that thrived on gossip not spread that tidbit around?

And why was it making her so angry?

And why was *that* making Cassandra so angry right on back?

The other woman stood so fast her chair fell over behind her.

"Do you think just because I run a coffee shop that I get every piece of news that this town has to give?" she countered. "Do you think that everyone in this town runs to *me* like I'm a bartender and tells me everything?"

"Yes!"

Cassandra stood firm.

"No!" she exclaimed. "They don't. I had no idea that Beth fought with Mr. Grant, and even if I had, it's not like I know to tell you every single little detail. Who do you think you are and who do you think *I* am? I mean, is that what you and your sheriff think of me? Do you really think I need to tell you every little piece of information I hear? Every little detail? And even if I did, am I supposed to remember everything I see and hear?"

Blake had apparently hit a nerve. Cassandra was fuming. She walked around the desk, anger in every movement.

"The last time you two barged in here, I was nice," she continued. "I was polite. I told you about Missy, about her mood, her personality, her laptop with the little panda sticker, what I thought about her death, and did all of that without anyone forcing my hand. Now you come in here, hanging up my phone to vent to me about—"

"Panda sticker?" Blake interrupted.

Cassandra looked ready to fight even harder at the rudeness but stopped. She must have noticed the shift in Blake's tone.

"Yeah. Missy's laptop had a little panda sticker on it," she said a moment later. "I only noticed it because it was covering the logo."

Blake's mind stalled for the second time since walking into the coffee shop. She didn't explain to the second person either what had caused it.

She turned on her heel and went back out into the hallway. Cassandra's footsteps hurried behind her.

"You're just going to yell at me and leave?" she asked. "Why? What's wrong?"

Blake didn't answer her. She didn't answer Corrie's questioning look from behind the counter either. There were only two people she acknowledged.

"Sorry, I'm going to have to cancel this time," she told Kyle, his face nothing but confused. She didn't wait around to explain more.

Instead, the second person she acknowledged came to her side without a word.

Liam followed her to the truck and had it started, no explanation needed. Even when Blake asked for him to drive them to her house, he did so without follow-up.

There was police tape still across the back door, but it had been repaired, so it was still locked when they searched the house to make sure no one was inside. Then Blake went with purpose to the guest bedroom that used to be her sister's study.

She went to the desk, took a key from the top drawer and unlocked the side bottom one with it. She set her eyes on a panda sticker covering a logo.

Before she did anything, she finally gave Liam an explanation.

"After going through all the paperwork and legal things it took to adopt the kids, to take over the house and to sort out her life insurance and get my head around all the new bills, accounts and leftover debt, I let the easier stuff rest." Blake waved a hand through the air. "This room became where I put things I wanted to look at more closely when life settled down. A few months ago, I had a burst of inspiration and decided to come in and finally start combing through Beth's things and boxing up what I wanted to save and donating what I thought she would be okay with."

She reached into the bottom drawer and put the object she was aiming for on the desktop.

Her finger traced the panda sticker on the laptop's cover.

"Cassandra said that Missy's laptop had this same sticker covering the logo. I'd almost feel like waving it off as a coincidence, but *this* particular sticker is a one of a kind. I know because Beth sent me a picture of it after she made it. For *her* laptop."

"Her laptop," Liam repeated.

Blake nodded.

"A few months ago I came in here and the laptop wasn't where I remembered putting it," she said. "I thought maybe I had just been distracted last time, but now I think it definitely had been moved. That would have been around the time Missy died. She—or someone else—could have put it back before her death."

Blake clapped, finally having two pieces of their very confusing puzzle attach.

"We've been having a hard time finding Missy's laptop because it wasn't hers to begin with."

Liam's voice was low, and it rumbled deep. If she hadn't already come to the same conclusion, she would have gotten chills at the new turn of events.

"The laptop we've been looking for was Beth's."

Blake nodded again.

"And whatever is on it was important enough that Missy must have been sneaking around here the day she died, and who else knows when."

Liam came around to her side. He looked down at the electronic as if it might answer.

"But why? What's the connection between Missy and Beth?"

Blake hadn't had the mental space yet to really think about that. Had there been any crossover between Missy and Beth? Just like Kyle, Blake felt the discrepancy between what she should have known and what she did know about her sister.

"I didn't even know Missy," Blake thought out loud.

"Other than what was in the papers or Lola told me. Which was about her death and the accident—"

"The accident at the steel mill," Liam interrupted, "where, according to Theo, Missy's friend Hector Martinez was almost killed by the furnaces overheating."

Adrenaline surged through Blake's entire being.

"Which is the accident that Beth investigated. Kyle just told me that Beth had a loud fight with Mr. Grant at the steel mill about some safety suggestions regarding the furnaces. Her car accident happened after she left that day. Everyone assumed she had gone to the steel mill that day to finish some paperwork. I never heard that she talked to—let alone yelled at—Mr. Grant."

Blake's mind was spinning.

She whipped her head up to stare into his eyes.

"What if that's what Missy was doing with the laptop? What if Missy was looking into Hector's accident? What if that's what actually caused her death? And, if any of that's true, what does that mean about Beth? Did she find something she shouldn't have during her investigation at the steel mill? And if she did, does that mean that her death wasn't an accident either?"

Had someone killed Beth to keep her quiet?

Had the same someone killed Missy?

Blake didn't know when it happened, but Liam's hand was over hers. The pressure felt grounding in a way.

His words even more so.

"Don't worry. No matter what, I'm going to take care of this."

Chapter Eighteen

The laptop didn't appear to have anything of note on it. At least none that were accessible to them. Half of the files were locked and encrypted and fell under the name of Beth's former job. Though none of them were labeled as Grayton Steel Mill.

"From what the press release after Hector Martinez's accident said, it was caused by human error," Blake had said, not for the first time since they had gone through Beth's laptop. They had also paid more attention to the details of Beth's former office, looking through materials Blake had yet to organize.

Liam had never really known Beth Bennet, but he got the feeling that she had been against bringing her work home with her. They had only found a few papers that seemed to be work-related. The rest were mailer odds and ends and things pertaining to the kids.

"A claim that Hector didn't dispute," Liam pointed out. "Not even his mother who took him with her back up north tried to make anyone believe otherwise."

Blake was still staring at the laptop.

They had been at it for over an hour since arriving at the house. In that time Blake had seemed to settle a little. Or had at least started masking all the emotions she must have been going through better than she had.

Liam didn't want her to have to hide anything from him, but he also understood that sometimes you needed time to process new information, and usually, that was easier with a clear head. Even if you had to temporarily force it clear to get there.

"But for Beth to publicly scold Mr. Grant?" Blake shook her head. "There must have been something that upset her about what she found during her investigation into the furnaces. She wasn't the type to just fly off the handle, especially not at a man like Mr. Grant. He holds more weight in this town than the mayor or the—" She stopped short.

Liam snorted.

"Or the sheriff," he finished. "Believe me, I may not be a true local, but I know the social standings of everyone. If Missy's dad has a loyal following for his old tractor supply business, the man who employs half of the town is close to God."

She nodded.

"Small towns give you a run for your money, that's for sure."

They had already gotten caught in the same questions before, just as they had with questions about Missy.

Why had Missy had Beth Bennet's laptop the day of her death? Had she broken into the Bennet home to get it? But then, if she had, why return it?

And did all roads lead back to the steel mill?

Liam ran a hand down his face, then stood. He extended his hand back down to where Blake was sitting. He had her on her feet in a blink.

"We need answers, so let's ask the right people questions," he said. "Looks like we're going to the steel mill."

THE PLAN SEEMED SIMPLE, but it took two hours on the phone to get an appointment set up to speak to Mr. Grant himself the next day. And even though Liam wanted to be the one taking the job on, it was Blake who ended up making the plans.

"Mr. Grant will see me faster than he will you," she had explained before calling. "He knows my father and I can play the sympathy card too. I'll just say I found something about my sister's investigation there and had some questions. He'll have to see me one way or the other."

And that's exactly what had happened.

Mr. Grant's assistant had confirmed the appointment for the next afternoon at his office. Like meeting with Kyle, Liam hadn't liked the idea of her going alone.

To which she had responded with a slight teasing to her tone.

"You're coming too, so don't worry about that. We just need to figure out how to get you in there without making anyone clam up."

That had been on his mind too but shifted to the back burner as day turned to night. They returned to Price's house and Liam relieved him. They spoke at the car after dinner was finished and before he left.

"Darius is still working on getting that guy with the baseball cap that y'all caught at the house to talk," he updated him. "He has a lawyer though and isn't budging. Then there's the whole Mater situation. Ray too."

Ray McClennan had flatlined twice and was still in the ICU. Mater was still in the hospital but wasn't saying a word either. Liam didn't like their only lead being the steel mill, but as the shadows of night grew darker, he couldn't think of another way to get an answer. At the very least, they could cross off some of their new questions.

Liam was still going over those questions as he took a new

change of clothes into the guest bathroom downstairs when soft footsteps sounded in the hallway. He peeked his head out to see Blake shuffling across the hardwoods toward him.

Since meeting the woman, he had been aware of her—from the lobby of the high school to the coffee shop to the department to her home to his apartment—but now it was like every sense Liam had went on a higher alert.

Her hair was wet from the shower she had taken after supper. It made the normal red into a dark heat, waving to the tops of her shirt and making the fabric darker too for it. Her shirt was oversized and swallowed her body all the way to her thighs. He could just make out the bottom of some shorts but only barely so. Then those legs were free and clear until the pair of socks that were helping her slide so quietly along the floor.

She had no make-up on. No lip anything.

Those lips.

They still hadn't talked about the kiss from earlier that day.

He wasn't going to bring it up now.

Blake had the baby monitor in her hand.

She shook it in the air a little when she met his eye.

"Unlike the three of them up there, I can't sleep," she said, voice low. "I was coming down to see if you wanted to chat."

Blake eyed the clothes in his hand.

"Oh, you're going *into* the shower. Not out." Her face fell. "I can wait. Or, well, I guess you might want to get some sleep, so maybe I'll just talk to you tomorrow."

Maybe it was because of that kiss that they weren't talking about, or maybe it was because, in that moment, something happened that had never happened before.

Blake Bennet looked lost.

Holding a baby monitor in her pajamas, hair wet, and

wanting to talk, Blake looked tired and lonely and restless. It was a combination that Liam knew well. She wanted someone next to her.

And Liam wanted to be that person for her.

So he reached out and took her hand, pulled her gently with him into the bathroom and then shut the door behind them.

BLAKE WAS HOLDING on to the baby monitor like it was a lifesaver and she had just been thrown into the sea without a hope of treading water.

Liam locked the bathroom door and put his folded clothes on top of the closed toilet seat. Then, like it was the most natural thing in the world, he reached past the shower curtain along the opposite wall and turned on the water.

When he turned back around to face her, Blake knew her face was the color of a stop sign.

He smirked. He pointed to the counter next to the sink.

"As long as you don't peek, you can sit there and we can chat while I shower," he said. "I wouldn't mind the company, if I'm being honest. It'll be nice to get out of my head for a little bit."

Blake opened her mouth. Then closed it. Then opened it again.

She didn't hate the idea, but was it appropriate?

You already kissed him earlier, what's talking to him in the bathroom? It's not like you'll be in the shower with him.

Her internal battle ended quickly.

She pretended to think about it a little longer, though, before making a big show of relenting.

"I guess we've already been through a firefight together," she said. "What's talking in the bathroom compared to that?"

Liam waited to undress after Blake settled on top of the counter. She closed her eyes just in time to see his shirt flutter to the ground. Her face went all flames at the sound of the rest of his clothes hitting the floor. She kept her eyes tight until the shower curtain moved twice. Even then she didn't open them all the way until he called out to her.

"You're safe."

Blake let out a little breath she had been holding and positioned the baby monitor so she could see it without holding on to it. She double-checked that her side was on Mute, and the other side was on Loud. They had brought the travel basinet for Bruce, so Lola and Clem were on the bed beside it, all three fast asleep. Blake envied their ability to sleep that easily. She had tossed and turned until she had needed to escape.

Though, did it count as escape if she had gotten out of bed with Liam in mind?

Running toward someone was its own plan after all.

"I was worried me walking around had woken you up," Liam said from the other side of the shower curtain. Blake glanced at it. She couldn't even see his silhouette. It would be a bold-faced lie if she pretended that didn't annoy her a little. "The only person I usually have to worry about waking up is Theo, and that boy can sleep through a bomb blast, I'm pretty sure. He's still upset that I wouldn't let him come stay with us, by the way. He said he's more than ready to fight if he needs to. I told him that's not needed."

Blake had originally wanted to talk more about their investigation but found her curiosity of the man overriding that never-ending circle of questions.

"You two must be close. He said you're like a babysitter to him?"

The sound of water shifted. Liam must have moved out of its spray a little.

"Yes and no," he said. "The first time I met him was in

the middle of a really nasty storm. His mom was out of town, and he lost his key and was huddled in the stairwell, scared out of his mind. I let him come to my place to wait out the storm. Almost two years later, and now he's at my place, eating my food, come rain or shine." Before Blake could ask about his parents, Liam added the answer on. "His dad passed away when he was a baby, and his mom remarried a guy who travels for work a lot and doesn't really like kids. His mom asked me to look after him one time, and after I said I would, she kind of stopped coming home regularly. It's kind of an unspoken thing that he can come and go as he likes. Just like it's an unspoken thing that he has to show me his grades, do chores, and stay out of trouble, or else." Liam laughed. "The first time I grounded him from TV because of his math grades was the last time he brought home bad math grades."

Blake smiled.

"Who knew the cold sheriff of Seven Roads had such a caring side?"

Liam snorted loud enough to be heard above the shower.

"Nice gossip travels slow, I suppose. It's much more fun to speculate about my divorce and lack of friends."

She nodded to that, though he couldn't see it.

"Lola said it's like hearing tires screech in the distance and waiting for the crash. Only to be kind of disappointed when it doesn't happen. Humans like a little chaos."

The sound of the water shifting let Blake know Liam was doing something different. She kicked her feet a little in the air and tried to keep her mind out of his space. A feat made easier by his next question.

"Speaking of Lola, you said she was your stepmom, right?"

Blake knew where this was going. It was touching in itself that Liam had held off bringing it up as long as he had.

"Yeah, she married my dad about ten years ago. They dated for a year or so before that. I didn't really know her all that well until I came back to Seven Roads." There was a silence. Blake addressed it with a chuckle. "Let me guess, you're trying to find a nice way to ask why she lives with us but my dad doesn't."

The sound of water shifted again.

"You got me," he admitted. He was quick to add on, "But you don't have to answer if you don't want to. It's not my business."

"As someone who is talking to you while you shower, I think we're past you not being a part of my business." It was meant to come off as a joke, but Blake faltered after saying it.

Would it really bother her for Liam to know this truth? One she hadn't told anyone ever before? One she hadn't *wanted* to tell anyone ever?

It wouldn't, she realized.

"When I was younger, my mom left," she started. "But even before that, I can't ever remember her and my dad getting along all that well. I think that's why he seemed to prefer Beth over me. I was, or am, my mom's twin. A carbon copy of her lookswise and, apparently, in the ways that we're stubborn." Blake sat up straighter. The wall was uncomfortable behind her but she made do.

"Dad and I butted heads a lot after that, but I thought that was pretty normal for single dads and their teenage daughters. But then the Mater thing happened, it was like it broke whatever was keeping the peace between us." Blake didn't say so, but she could never forget the way her father looked at her when he accused her of not knowing what loyalty meant. Still, at thirty-five, it made her heart upset a little. "I didn't stick around long after that. I wasn't even sure what I wanted to do in life when I left but eventually realized that the entire ordeal with Mater actually inspired me too. Out of everything that had happened, Sheriff Dean left an impression. Before I knew it, that was my goal. Fighting for justice with a badge on my chest."

She continued. "Dad, though, saw it as me rubbing salt in our old wound. I only saw him on holidays when I came home, and we both knew that was just to see Beth. As the years went by that became okay for me. I saw Beth, and after Dad married Lola, she'd reach out for him. That was enough for me. But then Beth passed away."

Blake looked down at her hands.

She felt wholly uncomfortable at the next part. Like getting pricked by several cactus needles but not knowing which one to take out first.

"When I first came back to deal with the funeral, Dad told me that life wasn't fair in taking her away. That she was the sweet one. The kind one. But me? I was the one in law enforcement, risking my life every day, dealing with violence. I was the one who didn't have a husband or kids. But Beth? It wasn't fair that the wrong daughter had died." Blake rubbed at her finger, eyes unfocused at the memory. "It wasn't fun to hear, but I agreed. I'd pick Beth to live too. Plus, this man had just lost his favorite kid. He could yell at me all he wanted, and I couldn't be mad, right? And then when he said it again after the funeral, I still believed that grief was powerful, and I only had to endure it for a while until he could get out of the shock of it all. I even held on to that belief when he said it again after I moved into Beth's house to take care of the kids."

Blake stopped rubbing her hand.

Her vision blurred a little.

She was embarrassed at the tears that threatened to come,

but for some reason, she felt like she had to finish the story for him. So she did.

"But then one day, Lola showed up. She had two suitcases, and my dad was nowhere to be seen. I knew it then, without her saying a word, what that meant. Dad wasn't just talking because he was hurt. He meant what he said. He wished it was me who had died, not Beth, and no matter how he looked at it, he couldn't get past it." Blake watched as a tear hit her leg. She was seeing Lola though. Standing at the end of the driveway, looking a world of sorry for her. "Lola never said it. Not out loud. She's kind like that. Instead, she asked if she could stay with us to help for a while, and when I tried to turn her away, she just walked past me and went inside. She hasn't left my side since, and my dad hasn't shown up either."

Blake laughed.

"For a family who's good at leaving each other, it sure hits different when outsiders just decide to stay. That's why—"

She hadn't heard the water stop or the shower curtain move to the side.

She hadn't seen him get out or wrap the towel around his waist.

She hadn't seen or heard him move to the spot right in front of her.

Blake, however, felt Liam's hand cup the side of her face and gently move her gaze up to his.

And for the kiss he pressed against her lips right after? Everything else in the world disappeared in an instant.

Then there was just Liam Weaver.

Chapter Nineteen

Liam pulled her to the edge of the counter, closer to him. It forced her legs to make a choice—block him or accommodate him. Blake chose the latter.

She wrapped her legs around him and his towel so there was no space left between them. Not that there was any to begin with up top.

Liam's kiss had lost its surprise. Now it had given way to something else.

Something heated.

Blake opened her mouth to let him in and Liam gladly accepted the invite. His tongue swiped inside as one of his hands tangled up into the back of her hair. He lightly pulled so her head tilted back. It made it easier to consume her that way, she decided. Because even with her up on the counter and him standing, his impressive height was still very much there.

Much like what she had felt that morning when she had been the one to kiss him.

She wanted him.

She didn't know why exactly, but she did.

She *wanted* him.

And she wanted him to want her.

Which she now knew, considering she could feel him through his towel, the desire was mutual.

With one arm fastening her against him and the other hand holding her head, Blake decided to do some positioning of her own. She let her hands blindly explore the wet body of the man against her, trailing his chest and back until she decided that it wasn't fair that he was the only one so exposed.

Blake pushed against him hard enough to let him know she wanted to stop.

Maybe it was too hard.

Liam not only stopped; he took two steps away from her.

His lips were red and swollen, his face was flushed, his expression was turning to apologetic.

"I—I'm sorry," he said uneasily. "I just think you're the most incredible woman I've ever met, and it was driving me crazy not to—"

He cut himself off, stopping amid his frazzled statement.

Probably because Blake had just thrown her shirt off from over her head and tossed it on the floor.

For a moment, Liam reminded her of a teenage boy. His eyes dropped dramatically, landing on her bra. That gaze didn't flinch as she undid said bra and let it hit the floor too.

"Turn the shower back on," she ordered, breathless but proudly still in control. "Then prove to me how incredible you think I am."

That shy, inexperienced teenager facade absolutely died on spot.

Liam was nothing but all man as he whirled around, turned the water on, and then came back to her. His lips crashed into hers while his hands did work.

One steadied her, the other slid beneath her shorts and underwear and expertly pulled both down in another fluid movement. No sooner were they on the floor than his towel joined them.

Then it was just Blake and Liam pressed against each other with nothing in between.

Still, Blake wanted to explore.

Liam was now the accommodating one.

With one arm, he helped guide her into the shower, not once breaking their stride. The back wall of it was cool to the touch, the water above them was warm.

When Liam finally made his way inside of her, Blake felt nothing but blessed heat.

By the time they left the shower, the water had long turned cold.

HIS HIP HURT.

Liam didn't mind. The pressure against his leg in the dark more than made up for any discomfort. Blake's even breathing let him know that she was still asleep. She seemed to be comfortable too. Her leg and arm were thrown across his and his chest. Her head was on her pillow, but her hair was fanned across his shoulder.

He smelled his own shampoo on it.

He couldn't help but smile at that.

The sun hadn't yet risen, and the only small source of light was coming from the baby monitor on the nightstand next to him. He wondered if someone on that end had been what had woken him, but a quick look showed that all three people, young and old, were still asleep in the room next door.

He started to wonder if he'd simply just woken when a noise pulled his attention farther across the nightstand.

It was his phone.

Someone was calling him.

Liam picked the phone up off the table so the vibrating wouldn't wake Blake. With as much care as he could, he detangled from the sleeping woman and hurried downstairs.

By the time he was confident he hadn't woken anyone, the call went to voicemail. Instead of checking it, he called the number right back.

Price answered on the first ring.

"Sorry if I woke you, Sheriff," he said in greeting. "But I think we might need you."

Liam glanced at the time on his phone. It was just after four.

"What happened?"

The sound of movement shifted between them before he responded.

"A few minutes ago, there was a shooting at the hospital. Ray McClennan is dead."

Liam was wide awake now.

"What?"

"There were no other causalities or injuries. The guy walked into the ICU and shot Ray quick. Then he rabbited before the security guards on duty could do a thing. Now the whole hospital is a mess."

Liam was walking back up the stairs but kept his voice low.

"Any idea who the shooter was?"

"Deputy Little is on scene and said that so far, she can't find anything that identifies him. Getting a statement from the staff is kind of chaotic too. Before he bolted, the gunman made a mess of the ICU. I can head there now or do you want me to—"

"Come here and watch the house," Liam finished for him. "If Ray was targeted, I want to see by who, but I'm not leaving this place unprotected."

If he was abusing his power to use one of his deputies as protection for Blake, he didn't care. Price must not have either. He agreed and said he would be there soon.

The call ended just as Liam was thinking about where he

had left his work clothes. He found them when the lamp next to the bed flicked on. There was a pillow imprint on the side of Blake's face. However, her eyes were sharp.

There was no reason or need to withhold the truth from her, so Liam bowled right in with it.

"There was a shooting at the hospital. Ray McClennan is dead. I need to go help with the aftermath and manhunt. Price is on his way here until I can come back. I'll have my phone on me, but if you can't get a hold of me for whatever reason, Price will help find me."

Blake was quick.

She was out of bed in a flash. To his surprise it was to hand him his shirt.

"I'll make you a quick cup of coffee. Price too." She was absolute speed-pulling on her own jeans and hurrying out of the room.

It wasn't until he was fully dressed and downstairs that he took a moment to think about the night before.

After they had shared more than a few moments in the shower, they had settled into the bed in a contented quiet. They hadn't yet talked about the two of them. About what their time together then meant for the future. If the stress of everything had made them impulsive. If, when they finished with the investigation and the need for close proximity ended, they would still want to be close to each other.

They didn't talk at all.

They just slept, holding on to each other.

Now didn't seem like the right time to talk about it either. So they didn't.

Blake handed him a coffee and told him to be safe.

Price showed up soon after, and together they told Liam not to worry.

Yet, as he drove away from the little house, now all lit up, he couldn't help but feel a new weight pressing down hard against his chest.

He didn't want to leave them.

And, only later in hindsight would he realize that he shouldn't have.

THERE WAS A lot of movement at the hospital. That didn't slow once the sun came up, and it didn't slow by the time shift change happened. Liam became the man in charge at the scene and directed his deputies in a search for the gunman. Then he helped Darius Williams speak to Ray's mother.

Doc Ernest helped her when she broke down in tears.

Ray's father was absent.

The security footage didn't help anyone. The man wore a mask, had been fast, and had known exactly where he was going.

"He targeted Ray," Liam had said to Darius while both standing outside of the security room.

The detective had nodded.

"Now I think we might know why our dear Glenn isn't saying a word," Detective Williams said.

Glenn Lowell had been the man in the baseball cap who had broken into Blake's home. Although he had finally given up his name, he had refused to explain anything else. Considering he was from a small town in Alabama and seemingly had no connection to anyone involved, his presence was still a mystery. One that now he might be more inclined to keep unsolved.

"It could be the fourth guy, the bald man in the rain jacket, tying up loose ends," Darius had added. "Ray didn't have any law attached to his bed because of the state he was in. Mater had Deputy Little outside of his room. So maybe he went for the easier target."

Still, it didn't sit quite right for Liam.

"Killing him seems like an extreme consequence, but for what?" Liam had asked. "The chance that they might talk about their plan for why they broke into the Bennet house?"

Darius had shrugged.

He still didn't know the whole story or about the laptop connecting Missy and Beth together. Liam was about to let him in when Liam was called to the hospital front desk.

He went there, for a moment thinking it might be Blake, when instead he was met with a stone-faced and determined teenaged boy.

The boy didn't waste any time.

"I need to talk to you," he said. "In private."

Liam quirked an eyebrow.

"And who are you?"

The teen lifted his chin a little. Liam noticed his eyes were a little swollen.

"My name's Cooper. Cooper Han."

Liam did the mental math fast. He was the best friend of Chase McClennan.

"I need to talk to you," Cooper said again. "Now, please."

Liam said okay and directed them to the closest, most private area they could find. They sat on either side of a small table next to a cluster of vending machines. Liam could tell the boy was serious, but he could also tell he was nervous.

Still, the nerves didn't win.

He got straight to the point.

"I hid Chase McClennan away, and I'm not telling anyone where he is until you arrest the man who killed Ray and the man who told him to do it."

Liam was gobsmacked.

"Come again?"

Cooper didn't back down.

"While Chase made a mistake listening to Ray during the car chase, nothing that has happened has been his fault," he said. "He just fell into his cousin's problems and didn't know how to get out. So I decided to take him out of all of this until all you professionals get it fixed. You can't see or talk to him until I know it's safe."

A part of Liam admired the conviction and obvious care. The other part, the sheriff taking the demands of a teen without any background information, wanted more to go on.

"The car chase? When you say he fell into Ray's problems, what do you mean? Does Chase know who killed Ray? And you said there's someone else behind that gunman? Does Chase know who?"

Despite his nerves, Cooper seemed to have come prepared for the questions.

"Ray was the one with all of the answers, Chase doesn't know anything."

Liam tilted his head to the side a little in disbelief.

"Then why would he be in danger if he doesn't know anything? Because, to me, it seems like Chase and Ray shared some anger, and that anger somehow got to me and maybe even one of my friends. Now that anger has led to a murder and I'm still trying to put all the pieces together to make sure nothing else bad happens. How can I do that? How can I protect anyone if I don't even know who I'm protecting them from?"

This question stumped the boy. His brow knitted together, he bit at his bottom lip. Then, that resolution that had demanded the sheriff to do his job all at once disappeared.

Cooper balled his fists and squeezed his eyes shut. His words came out quick but clear.

"Chase isn't the one who knows anything. It's me. I'm the one who told him about the code, and Ray's the one who overheard me do it. I'm the one who started this. I'm the one who—"

Liam froze.

His question didn't.

"The code?" he interrupted. "What code?"

Cooper opened his eyes. He looked pained again, but his answer was as clear as day.

"The code that I gave to Missy before she died."

Chapter Twenty

Price was upset. He made that clear. Blake made it even clearer that she wasn't going to lose her chance to get some answers.

"Listen, this isn't my first rodeo," she told him, swinging into the open car door. "I'm Sheriff Trouble remember? I should be able to handle talking to Mr. Grant senior."

Price wasn't so sure.

Just as he hadn't been sure the first time she had told him she had received the call from Mr. Grant's assistant that the meeting needed to be moved up or canceled until further notice.

"At least let me touch base with the sheriff first," he said, not for the first time. "I gave him my word that I'd keep the house safe, and now part of that house is leaving by herself. Let me just call Darius and see if he can't find him."

Blake rolled her eyes.

"Listen, Price, I appreciate the concern. So much so that I'm going to skip over the fact that it feels like you need his permission to let *me* do what I want and instead ask you very sweetly to continue keeping my family safe." She motioned to the car. "This is the only thing I can do for my family right now—try to get some answers—so let me go before I'm late and the almighty Mr. Grant decides he doesn't want to talk anymore."

Price looked like he wanted to keep arguing.

He also looked like he understood it was pointless.

Sheriff Trouble, who he had initially admired, had her mind made up. And, what's more, Lola had already backed her up once Blake had told her the entire truth about everything they had learned over the last week or so. With two fierce women going against him, he had little room to do anything other than protest.

"Keep your phone on," he finally said, relenting. "If anything feels off or weird, call immediately. And I'll track the sheriff down while you do it. So don't be surprised if he shows up grumpy that you left without him."

"Understood."

AND THAT WAS how Blake found herself alone at the steel mill.

Grayton Steel Mill was on the largest plot of commercial land that Seven Roads had to offer. It was a collection of warehouses, offices, storage rooms and production lines that expanded such a distance that some workers used buggies to drive around from place to place. The main office was the largest office buildings, mainly due to the cafeteria housed inside and the second floor corporate offices.

It was on that second floor that Mr. Grant was waiting for her.

Blake parked, made sure her phone's ringer was on loud, and struck out across the parking lot. As she walked, she hoped Liam was okay. She knew all too well how stressful the job could be, never mind when it came to a case that had personally touched you. That was another reason Blake wanted to get this over with.

She wanted answers for herself, Beth and Missy.

She also wanted them for Liam.

He had been targeted, he had been hurt, and Blake didn't want that to happen again.

Not to her man.

Her face heated a little at the last thought. It had sprung up so suddenly she didn't know how to dissect it.

Thankfully, she was distracted away from it.

Someone was calling her name. Or, rather, an old name.

"Sheriff Bennet!"

Blake turned to see a surprising face running up to meet her. "Theo?"

Theo was wearing coveralls and a name tag. He was smiling ear to ear.

"What are you doing here?" he asked. He made a show of looking behind her. "Is Liam with you? I heard about the shooting at the hospital, but he didn't answer when I called."

"He's still there working, I think. I'm here to talk to Mr. Grant. We have an appointment. Why are *you* here?"

Theo tapped his name tag.

"I have a part-time job in the cafeteria. I usually work the weekend shifts. You caught me on my lunch break. I was just about to head out." His smile brightened even more. "Here, I'll take you up to his office. I've been there a few times before, delivering meals."

Blake accepted the help simply because, of all of the places she had been in Seven Roads, Mr. Grant's office had never been one of them.

"I didn't even know Mr. Grant was in today," he said as they walked. "He must have parked in the private lot behind the building. Him and his son are the only ones who really use that though. It floods something wicked when it rains."

"So, his son, Elijah, does actually work a lot, huh?" she asked. "I heard he's won over workers because he pulls his weight."

They had entered the lobby, so Theo lowered his voice. Though his snort was easy to hear.

"He works, yeah, but Elijah Grant walks around this place like he's some kind of god when his dad isn't around. You should feel the vibe of the workers in the cafeteria when he's nearby versus when he's not. A total mood shift."

He led them up some stairs to a second smaller lobby. There was no one behind the desk, but Theo went to check it anyway.

"Are you sure you're supposed to meet Mr. Grant today?" he asked. "I know sometimes he'll work during the weekend shifts, but it doesn't look like Rhonda's here. She's his personal assistant. Do you have the time right?"

Blake was about to check her phone again when the door down the hall to their right opened.

The man was tall, wore a crisp business suit and didn't skip a beat at the sight of them.

"Mr. Grant," Theo said in greeting.

Mr. Grant?

He was all smiles as he walked over to them.

"Oh, sorry, I thought you had an appointment with Grant Senior," Theo said. He didn't bother to lower his voice. The man approaching laughed.

"I realized after the fact that my assistant might have confused you with that." He looked to Blake and extended his hand. "You must be Blake Bennet. I'm Elijah Grant Junior. I'm the one who made the appointment with you since my father is out of town on business."

Red flag.

It sprung up quickly.

Blake shook his hand with grace.

"Oh, that's no problem. Maybe you can help me too. If you don't mind, that is. I'm sure you're a busy man."

Elijah Grant.

Blake didn't know much about him other than he was Mr. Grant's only child. Even though his father's company employed half the town, he had never been one to fraternize in the social aspects of Seven Roads. Elijah was a few years older than Blake, but she knew he hadn't attended any of Seven Roads's schools either. She wasn't even sure she had been in the same room with him in any of her thirty-five years of living.

Yet, she was good at reading people.

She had a strong feeling that Elijah wasn't as nice as his smile.

But neither was Blake.

She turned to nod to Theo. The boy was looking between them with not-so-sure eyes. Blake tapped his hand in what she hoped was a casual way.

"Thanks for walking me here," she said. "Make sure you give your dad a call and tell him you were kind enough to show me around. He'd be proud of your manners."

Blake was, of course, talking about Liam. While she was fine to go talk to Elijah in private, the change was enough to make her feel the need to update Liam. She was still ready to handle herself, and even if she hadn't been, leaving now might spook the man. How and why, she wasn't sure, but Blake did know that he had heard her request and accepted it instead of his father.

And that made her mighty curious.

Thankfully, Theo played his part cool.

"I'll let him know," he said. "I was just about to call him anyways since it's my break. Y'all have a nice chat. I'll be going now."

She imagined if he had a hat, he would have tipped it to them.

He cast her a quick look, and she returned the gesture with her own little nod.

Elijah seemed wholly unaware of their secret exchange. He swept his hands in the direction of his office with a smile still hanging on his lips.

"This way."

He wasn't the CEO of the company and it showed. Elijah's office was only big enough to fit a desk, a love seat, and a coffee table. His view wasn't the greatest either. It faced the mill instead of the front view of trees and a nicer landscape of the town. There was also the metal roof of the first floor that was right outside the window. Storm debris and rust patches sat along its creases. There was also a damp smell that met Blake's nose as she was guided into the lone chair opposite his desk.

All in all, it didn't seem to fit the man wearing a suit on a Sunday.

"Sorry again for the misunderstanding," Elijah began. "Rhonda, my father's assistant, will contact me if there's business after hours or on the weekends so as to give my dad some space. When the request came in for you to talk to him, it came to me first. I felt like I was just as capable of answering, and, well, she said there sounded like there was some urgency there too."

Blake decided to play it sweet for a while. She upped her southern twang and made sure to smile nice.

"Well, I sure do appreciate you taking the time to see me, especially on the weekend and on such short notice. You must be plenty busy as it is."

That seemed to stroke his ego just right.

His shoulders relaxed as he sat forward and domed his fingers together.

"I'm just happy to be of help. I heard you wanted to talk about your sister, Beth Bennet?"

Blake was curious as to how much Elijah actually knew

of what happened. She watched his expression closely as she spoke.

"Yes. I recently heard that Beth had a fight with your father about the safety investigation she performed here on the Hector Martinez incident. I know it's none of my business, especially if it was about work, but it happened to be the day she passed, and, well, I've been trying to get a better idea about my sister's life leading up to her last days. So I thought I'd ask your father what that fight might have been about, especially since it's so unusual for Beth to get heated."

Elijah was as cool as a cucumber. No surprise.

"Ah, yes, I remember the fight. Though it was more of a misunderstanding. She thought my father had disregarded her suggestion for a several-step authentication system for the furnaces' computer system. *In reality* it was me who went in a different direction." He swapped out his smile for a look of concern. "My father was trying to explain I had already implemented a new security system that would take care of any future human-caused errors."

If he had stopped right there, if he had ended his side at that moment, then Blake might have wavered in her initial thought of the man. She might have questioned if Missy's ex, Kyle, had seen the end of the fight instead of just the yelling. Then, realizing she had never asked, felt a bit guilty and frustrated that she hadn't thought to at the coffee shop the day before. She would have felt a sliver of negligence, all her fault.

But Elijah kept talking.

"I was ready to personally reach out to her to explain the situation, but, well, I never got the chance."

It was a simple statement and understandable. He couldn't have talked to Beth about the change because Beth had had her accident right after.

It made sense.

However, Blake had made a career of reading people. Of following her gut.

He'd met her on the weekend instead of his father. It didn't feel like an obligation.

It felt like Elijah Grant wanted to talk to her for his own reasons.

So she kept going to see which one of them would get what they wanted first.

"I guess you can explain it to me, then?" she asked sweetly. "I mean, I don't know a lot about computers, or anything really about them, but it sounds like you do. I'm sure my sister would have loved to hear it."

Elijah's smile lifted.

It wasn't like Liam's at all. Liam's made her feel warm. This man's made her feel like she had just accidentally touched something wet while using public transportation.

He waved his hand through the air, all nonchalance.

"I won't get into the specifics, but the new system that's in place is all automated, minus a few initial commands."

"Automated? The furnaces can run on their own?"

"Once set up and given specific times to run, yes," he said. "We still need people to man them, but now we don't have to worry about people like Mr. Martinez getting hurt during their maintenance."

"But he wasn't hurt during their maintenance." The words came out as Sheriff Bennet instead of coy Blake before she could stop them. She tried to save face in the next breath. "I mean, I heard that Hector's accident was him trying to manually shut them down after one started overheating. He was worried the whole warehouse might go if one had a meltdown and that the entire mill would be affected. That's the word around town at least."

That part was partially true. The rumor mill had split between Hector being negligent and Hector trying to be a hero. The negligence story had gained more traction after the steel mill sent out the press release about his accident being human error. That's why Beth had been sent in after all.

Elijah took the barb without emoting anything other than coolness.

"Mr. Martinez made a judgment call that was sadly not a call he should have made at all. We had many safety protocols in place to facilitate a solution that would have been safe and effective. Instead, Mr. Martinez put his own life in danger and paid dearly." Once again, if Elijah had stopped there, a seed of doubt might have sprouted within Blake. Yet the man couldn't help himself. This time, though, the addition cost him.

"In fact, the person in charge of the safety protocol put in place is here today. I thought maybe you might be interested in talking to him."

Blake felt the familiar rush of adrenaline flood her system. The red flag that had sprouted was now in a forest of them.

To think, after everything she had been through in the last week, she had walked willingly into the final boss's lair.

Because in that moment, Blake was sure she was talking to none other than the man behind Missy's death and behind her sister's accident. And who very much wanted to add Blake's death to the list.

But why wait?

Why not kill her on sight at her house? Why not go in guns blazing to take her out? Why make an appointment to sit down and talk to her? Why ask questions? What could he want? What could—

Missy's flash drive and Beth's laptop.

But nothing of note had seemed to be on Beth's laptop.

So that left the code on the flash drive.

Blake wasn't sure where it fit exactly, but she bet her life that it was this man's downfall.

"Oh, that would be nice," she said to his offer. Though it was less of an offer and more of a warning. He had already texted something on his phone. "But, first, I have one last question, if you don't mind."

Elijah met her eye with a new smugness.

"Sure. What do you have for me?"

She decided it would be impolite to keep pretending to be someone she wasn't.

So Blake dropped her smile and did something she had become quite good at during her career in law enforcement. She applied pressure where she thought she might break the man's no-doubt carefully applied facade.

"How angry were you after you realized Missy hid her flash drive with the code before you killed her?"

It was like wiping red marker off a white board.

That fake politeness was no match for the burn of his rage.

Blake's shot in the dark had landed. And it had hit a bulls-eye to boot.

But he wasn't the only one shooting.

The door to the office flung open. Blake threw herself back, toppling over with her chair but managing to stay upright as she tried to scramble away from the new intruder.

However, the person who ran inside and immediately slammed the door closed behind him wasn't a no-name lackey.

It was Theo, and he was breathing heavy.

"Gunman outside!" he yelled. He whirled around and pointed to Elijah. "Gun in here!"

Blake was so startled by Theo's entrance she hadn't noticed that Elijah was reaching for something. Her body went on autopilot. She threw herself across the desk ready to disarm the man.

Everything after that seemed to go in double speed.

A gunshot.

Glass breaking.

Then chaos.

Chapter Twenty-One

Liam was pissed. At everyone.

He was angry at Cooper Han because the boy had waited so long to tell anyone about the code. It was only when someone he loved was threatened that he even dared come out to say a word. Though, Liam knew it counted that the teen had tried to correct his hesitance and had done so in the face of potential danger. So he couldn't hold on to that anger too long.

Which worked out, because next he became angry at Price.

Once he had finished his conversation with Cooper, he had noticed his calls weren't coming through or going out. That happened occasionally near the hospital and across a few other spots in town. Panic had risen through him in an instant, then anger came in swiftly on its heels once he finally spoke with Price, who explained what was going on with Blake.

Mr. Grant had changed his appointment time with Blake, and she had simply gone along with the flow.

Solo.

So then the anger at Price for letting her go had gone and attached to the stubborn woman who hadn't waited for him.

She hadn't even called him, only left a text saying where she was going. Nothing else.

At that point Liam had already been in the truck and heading over to the steel mill as fast as the wind.

Then he had gotten a call from Theo.

Normally, he would have sent the call to voicemail if he thought he was heading into danger and needed to focus, but the timing of the call was too coincidental.

Liam had answered on the second ring.

He didn't have time to say hello. Theo was rattling off information fast.

"Sheriff Bennet is at the steel mill talking to Elijah Grant, Mr. Grant's son, in his office. I think she was supposed to meet Mr. Grant instead, but something changed. Then she told *me* to call *my* dad and let him know that I had walked her in. Which I think she meant to call you and tell you."

Liam's anger had switched one more time.

Right onto Elijah Grant. The same man Cooper had just said had installed the code that everyone kept dying for.

"Find a way to let her know that Elijah is dangerous and then you both get out of there," Liam said, not bothering with the backstory. "I'm a minute or so away from the mill."

Bless him, Theo didn't ask any questions. He said okay and then started moving fast on his side of the phone.

All at once, that noise stopped.

His whisper was the loudest Liam had ever heard.

"The man who you said attacked y'all at the Bennet house but got away. Was he tall and bald?"

Adrenaline skyrocketed from the tips of Liam's toes all the way up to the ends of his hair.

"Yes."

"Then I think he's walking down the hallway and—and he has a gun!" The sound on Theo's end of the call wasn't still after that. He was all out yelling. "Second floor to the right. End of the hallway and—"

A loud *clatter* vibrated through the phone and across the silence of the cab of the truck. Liam looked at his phone to see the call was still going. He heard what sounded like running in the background.

Theo had dropped his phone.

Liam cussed and pressed the gas pedal to the floorboard.

The call ended right after that.

Liam cussed again.

He called back, but no one answered. By the time he made it to the parking lot and was out of his truck and running, he had already called in every able-bodied person from the McCoy County Sheriff's Department.

But he wasn't about to wait around for them.

Liam checked his gun as he ran through the parking lot and burst through the lobby doors of the main office. He took the stairs two at a time and put all of his attention on the hallway that led to the offices at the right end.

A cell phone was discarded on the tile halfway between him and the open door at the end of the hallway.

It was Theo's.

Liam stepped over it and kept his gun aimed straight ahead and ready.

Yet no one appeared.

Liam swung into the office and found it empty. He would have backtracked had he not noticed the windows.

One was broken. The other was opened wide.

Surely no one had gone out them…

He hurried to check. His stomach lurched at what he saw outside.

The metal overhang from the first story stretched across the full width of the building. It wasn't until midway across that the slope led to a flat roof that was connected to a storage building. There the roof was flat and easier to manage.

There he could just make out four figures, all moving fast.

Even at the distance, Liam could see Blake clearly.

As MUCH AS she didn't want to admit it, Blake was at a serious disadvantage.

Their rooftop escape might have worked had Elijah's helper not broken into the office the second that she had been able to disarm Elijah. Instead, the best she and Theo could do in the moment was flee through the window that had been shot out by accident.

She had let the boy lead the way, and again had the bald man not been right on their heels, they might have been able to scramble down the side of the current building they were on and make a run for it.

Instead, they had been cornered on a rooftop with two men both holding guns.

Blake extended her arms out as wide as she could and put herself firmly in front of Theo.

She was out of breath but managed to keep her voice steady.

"He doesn't know anything. Let him go and we can talk."

Elijah, who seemed to be struggling the most, laughed through his spurts of trying to regain his breath.

"You're—you're in no position to—to negotiate," he said. "We—we will talk though."

He lowered his gun after looking at the bald man at his side. The fourth man from the ambush at her home. He was unmoving as he kept his gun aimed at her.

"Tell me where—where it is," Elijah said, holding his side until breathing seemed to come easier. "Tell me where the flash drive is."

Blake shook her head.

"I do that and we're dead," she said. "Let him go, though, and I'll tell you whatever you want."

It was a bluff.

But it didn't matter. She knew neither man was going to let Theo or her go.

Now the best she could do was stall for time and hope that the boy had gotten her hint to call Liam.

If he had, then Blake didn't doubt for a second that the sheriff wasn't on his way to save them.

Elijah laughed, very much a man with no intention of letting them live.

"Do you know, the last person who tried to negotiate with me found herself at the bottom of a dried-up creek. I suggest what you focus on now is how easy to make this next part for the both of you. Because, believe me, I can make you suffer if I need to."

Blake narrowed her gaze.

"So you really did kill Missy Clearwater," she said.

The man rolled his eyes. It was an unbecoming sight.

"All I did was hit her a little. It's not my fault she took a tumble right after that. If she had simply listened to me and handed over that damned little flash drive, we would have been fine. But, no. All you women like playing hero. I think it's only poetic that you'll be the one to end the cycle, considering it was your sister who started it."

Blake lowered her arms. Theo was right at her back.

"Beth's car accident wasn't an accident," she stated.

"Beth's car accident wasn't an accident," Elijah confirmed. He snorted. "Though it was her fault, not ours. My friend here just wanted to talk about her findings. It isn't his fault that she got scared and started driving like a lunatic."

Blake's hands fisted.

If she hadn't been trying to shield the teen behind her, she would have lunged at the man. Instead, she tried to get answers.

"Which means that she *did* find something she wasn't supposed to."

Elijah was back to smug.

"Do you know how many safety inspectors we've had come out to the mill over the years? Do you know how many have turned a blind eye or taken money to overlook an infraction? But no. Not Beth Bennet. She was a woman who wanted to stick her nose where she shouldn't."

He laughed.

He actually laughed.

"Who knew that she was so fast? Squirreling away the one thing that could mess up everything?"

"Her laptop."

Elijah nodded.

"Since we couldn't find it anywhere after so many months, though, we thought that was that." He breathed out his annoyance. "Then Missy Clearwater, the beloved daughter of my father's best friend, used her name to start asking questions. Who did she even think she was? Acting like she had been the one hurt when it was just that good-for-nothing friend of hers Hector?" He shook his head. "Then suddenly *she* had the code and then, *then*, she had the audacity to try to bring my father into this whole thing? Trying to mess up my inheritance? I don't think so."

Elijah blew out another short huff of air.

"She should have known better. After the way this town treated her when her father decided to shut down their business? Can you imagine the flak I would have caught had they found out I was the one trying to burn this place down for a payout?"

Blake's mouth opened on its own accord.

Elijah saw the shock and seemed to revel in it.

"And there it is," he said, the smile from earlier returning.

"You can't fake that kind of surprise, Eric. Did you know that?" He patted the bald man's shoulder. His smugness was returning as well. He looked to Blake again. "I don't think Miss Bennet here knows as much as she's pretending to. Let's see. Miss Bennet, can you tell me what exactly the code is for? Or did you come here for a fishing expedition only?"

Blake hated that she didn't have a good answer.

She also hated that the feeling of dread in her had tripled.

Elijah had found out that she was more expendable than he had originally thought. Which meant they didn't have long.

Blake wished she could hear sirens in the distance.

She wished she had her gun.

She wished she hadn't come to the mill by herself.

She wished she had waited for Liam.

She wished that she could turn back time to them all sitting at the dinner table, Clem on his lap, Bruce in her arms, and Lola fussing over the food between them.

She wished she could hug the kids again. Kiss Liam. Laugh with Lola.

She wished she could tell her dad she was sorry that life for them had gotten so offtrack.

She wished she could hear her sister tell her to make sure she ate something yummy.

Instead, she was about to become another tragedy and trauma in Seven Roads history.

Or so she thought.

Movement caught the corner of Blake's eye just as it alerted the man with the gun trained on her, Eric. He whirled around and shot without waiting.

Blake didn't waste that time worrying about his target. She closed the distance between her and Elijah before he could lift his gun. Pain exploded along her fist as it connected with his jaw.

Another shot went off, then another, on the roof behind them.

Elijah's gun hadn't gone off yet, but it also hadn't fallen.

Blake struggled against him, throwing hits and kicks as hard as she could.

The man knew how to play dirty though. He slammed his head into Blake's so hard that all she could do was try not to pass out as she fell backward against the ground. Theo was already there, trying to pull her away.

He yelled something, but despite everything, Blake was getting tunnel vision.

That vision had Elijah at its center. He had his gun coming up to aim at her.

With everything she had left in her, Blake willed karma to see him pay for all the bad he had done.

A split second later, another boom sounded.

Elijah crumpled to the ground.

As darkness took her, Blake could only think of one word. *Good.*

Chapter Twenty-Two

The world was a lot nicer when Blake opened her eyes next. She had to admit that was probably mostly due to the man staring down at her.

Liam's gaze didn't waver.

"You know, I've been to war and been less stressed than I was today," he told her. "Being a loner, not talking to people? That's easy stuff. Falling for Sheriff Trouble? Hardest thing I've done yet."

Blake had questions, but her focus was watered down. She wanted to ask about that falling-for thing but was getting distracted by what was above his head.

"Where am I?"

Her throat hurt at the question. She flinched.

Liam's face softened. His fingers traced the side of her jaw before his hand enveloped her own at her side.

"You landed yourself in the hospital. We're in a private room. You just cleared a round of doctors."

Blake's brow scrunched of its own accord.

"Concussion?" she asked.

He nodded.

"And one heck of a bruise and bump for it." His face darkened. "Who knew Elijah Grant had such a damned hard head."

The name brought a bad taste into her mouth.

It wasn't the only thing.

"Did I get sick?" she asked. Blake felt like she was extremely hungover. He confirmed her suspicion.

"You came to in the ambulance and got sick a whole bunch. Poor Theo nearly lost it at the sight but didn't want me to tell you that." He smiled, lopsided. "He says he's not like most teenagers, but he really wants to keep that reputation of his tight."

Blake was relieved to see Liam joking about the boy.

"He's okay, then?"

He nodded. Then became serious again.

"I actually don't think I could have pulled off getting you to the ambulance without him. You're easy to carry under normal circumstances but off a building's roof—well, it was a bit trickier. Plus, he kept fussing after the stitches on my arm. They didn't pop, though, and he kept his cool."

Blake was trying to think back.

All she remembered was Elijah's head hitting hers.

That and his admissions. The old ache in her heart started to hurt. She decided to push it to the side for now.

"What happened?"

Liam held her hand tight as he recounted the rooftop fight. While she had taken on Elijah, he had made his way out onto the roof from the office and shot the man named Eric the moment he was close enough to get a good opening. Before he could knock the man out with a bone-crunching hit, Elijah had already attacked Blake.

"That's when you shot Elijah," she guessed.

She was wrong.

"Someone followed me and came out onto the rooftop too. He's the one who shot Elijah."

Blake didn't understand his expression. She raised her eyebrow in question.

"Who was it?"

She wasn't sure she heard him clearly, so she asked him to repeat himself.

The second time, it was clear enough.

"Ryan Reed, your sister's former brother-in-law. He's the one who shot Elijah."

"Ryan? As in Tim's brother? Clem and Bruce's uncle?" Blake didn't understand, so she had to make sure she clarified.

Liam nodded.

"Apparently he didn't leave town. A good thing too that he showed up. His shot was right on target." Liam squeezed her hand. "It was a kill shot too. Elijah Grant is dead."

For so many reasons, and probably more that she couldn't think of, this made Blake cry. Her tears were hot and big and made her head hurt even more.

Liam didn't say a word. Instead he kept her hand safe and secure within his until, a few minutes later, she stopped.

"We can talk about everything after you get some rest," he told her, wiping his thumb over her cheek. "Until then, I just want to ask you one question and one question only."

Blake was so drained. All she could do was nod.

Liam smiled.

"I'm sure there is a more suave way to do this, but the cold sheriff of Seven Roads sure doesn't know how to do anything but ask outright." He cleared his throat. "Blake Bennet, when you're feeling better, how about we go out on a date? Dinner, movies, playing in the park with the kids—I don't care what it is. As long as it's with you, I'll be happy."

Exhaustion momentarily paused.

Blake returned his smile.

"As long as we eat something yummy, I'm in."

A DAY PASSED before they finally got the rest of their answers. However, Blake ended up getting them from an unlikely source.

Ryan Reed was in handcuffs but sitting in the sunlight on a bench outside the hospital. He had already told his story to Detective Williams and Liam back at the department. Now it was her turn, thanks to Liam pulling some strings to make the conversation happen.

"Missy called me a month or so after Beth's death looking for my brother," he said, starting the story of why he had killed Elijah Grant. "You know Tim. Once he left Beth and the kids, he left any thought about this life behind. I tried to tell her it was useless to call him, and then, in the middle of all of that, she said it could be a matter of life and death, and she brought up Beth's accident. The way she said it... I couldn't shake it. Then she asked me to meet her since I was still family and maybe could talk to you."

He looked sheepish at that.

"She didn't hear that we had fallen out. About how much of an ass I made out of myself at the funeral. How out of line I was with you talking about the insurance money. I just couldn't believe how we'd all gotten there. I know I wasn't a rock star uncle, but Tim just up and leaving like that as a dad? And then Beth was just gone. No matter what, though, I shouldn't have done what I did. I'm sorry about it all, really I am. Guess I should have said that sooner."

He kept on without waiting to see if Blake accepted his apology or not.

"When we met, Missy told me everything, starting from the beginning. She wasn't suspicious about the steel mill or Elijah until after she heard about Beth's accident. That's why she went down the rabbit hole. Beth's death and, well, that friend of hers. That Hector fella." He shook his head. "She was sure as the sun shines that Hector wouldn't have made such a mistake with those furnaces. So she went to her daddy about it, who, in turn, asked Mr. Grant about it. I guess her questions got to Elijah in the end. And he wasn't appreciative of it. He met her at the mill, but she said he was acting weird. He kept asking for proof and if she'd been close to Beth."

Ryan sighed. It had dragged him down.

"Missy said that she snuck into the furnace room after that, saying she was visiting her boyfriend that worked out there. She didn't know what to look for but suspected it might have something to do with the computer. So she copied everything she could onto one of those flash drive things. Someone caught her doing it too."

That someone was Cooper Han. As part of his tech program, he had found Missy there during one of their tours fumbling around with the computer. If it hadn't been for his aversion to judging people without giving them a chance, he might have turned her in. Instead, he offered to help her.

"That boy is a far throw from the likes of me, I'll tell you that," Ryan said. "He was able to find some kind of code in all of that garble that shouldn't have been there. He can probably explain it better than I can, but they realized—as far as I can tell—it basically could make the furnaces overheat by themselves, eventually causing a catastrophic meltdown. He guessed it had been put in manually by someone to make everything melt down. But there was no way to figure out who."

"That's what happened with Hector," Blake realized. "He thought it was an error that caused the meltdown and tried to help. But it was on purpose."

Ryan nodded.

"Missy told Cooper to be quiet about it, worried it was dangerous information to have, and that's when she called me looking for Tim. She was trying to figure out if Beth had found the code during her investigation or if she had any info on her work laptop about it. I didn't have any idea but told her that if Beth had a laptop that it should be at the house with you." Ryan laughed. "So she actually went and stole it from you. I guess you were busy with the kids and didn't notice, but, sure as sure, she had it with her, trying to figure out if the code was there."

Blake couldn't believe it. Then again, maybe she could. Missy Clearwater had more than proven she was a clever girl.

"Then she told me she was putting it back, worried that if anyone found it on her, they might think you had a part in this. And she didn't want you or the kids in danger."

A look she couldn't decipher went across Ryan's face. He continued.

"I met with Missy the day she died. She said her father had gotten drunk the night before and wondered if his friend, Mr. Grant, was going to cash out of the steel mill while he could or give the massive debt to his son. She prodded her daddy until she got a better picture of the situation."

The situation, which they would later confirm through an investigation, was that the senior Mr. Grant had used a lot of his fortune to help pull his son Elijah out of severe debt before he'd come back to Seven Roads. It was only after Mr. Clearwater, his good friend, had sold his business to retire that he had started to think about letting his son inherit the mill, only to leave him strapped with the financial fallout.

Something that Elijah had found out about.

And tried to plan for.

"Elijah wanted the mill to burn down so he could collect the insurance payout. Simple as that," Ryan finished.

"So, did Beth even know about the code?"

Ryan shrugged.

"Missy never found out, and you know me, I'm not exactly book smart. The most I've done was try to figure out who all was connected to Elijah. I didn't want a one of them to escape."

Blake hurt for her sister. They would never know for certain if Beth had figured out what was going on, but Blake liked to think she had. That's why she had been so angry the day she had died. That's why she had been so scared when the man named Eric, a favorite employee of Elijah's, had come after her while driving that day.

Eric never said a word on the matter, but a security camera outside the hospital had caught him fleeing the scene after he killed Ray McClennan. Chase had become Ray's voice in the end, admitting that Elijah had paid Ray to try to stop Liam at all costs from digging into Missy's death. At the time, Ray had lied to Chase about what was happening, saying that the sheriff was a bad man who had done bad things. It was only after Cooper Han had heard what had happened that he had told his best friend Chase about the code.

He hadn't realized that Ray had been listening.

Or that Ray would raise the flag of alarm to Elijah, who had had no idea there was a code floating around out there somewhere. That's where the panic had come in and that's where he'd gotten sloppy.

He'd wanted Beth's laptop, sure she had a copy of the code. In his mind, the only way to get what he wanted was to use the kids to threaten Blake to find it. His panic had only ratcheted higher when Blake and the sheriff were seen around town together. He'd been sure they were looking for the code too.

So, in came Ray McClennan. A young man who had his own set of daddy issues. He'd been more than willing to do whatever for the youngest Grant.

Too bad for him that Elijah had always planned to frame

Ray for whatever misdeeds took place. They'd find that out later, when Glenn Lowell, the man in the baseball cap, finally opened up. The ambush at Blake's home had been Elijah's plan. The car chase had been Ray's bad makeshift first attempt after seeing the sheriff and Blake outside of the restaurant that Chase worked at by chance.

"All these seemingly smart guys sure made a lot of bad decisions, all because they were worrying about two women who were chasing the truth," Ryan said after a moment. "I went to tell you at the school gym that day, but I lost my nerve. I wish I hadn't. I wish I'd helped Missy even more."

Blake looked at Ryan with new eyes.

He looked right on back and was as serious as she had ever seen him.

"I know my brother wasn't a good husband or dad, and I'm really sorry for him. I'm also real sorry I didn't step up like you did. But I tried to make things right. As right as I could. From us. From Tim and me. Because Beth was a good, good woman. So was Missy. They both deserved a long, happy life. That's why I killed Elijah without an ounce of doubt in me, and that's why I'm not sorry for it."

He shook his head.

"Though, I suppose I am sorry for the trouble it might bring you and the kids in town. I'm sure Mr. Grant isn't going to be happy with our family after I killed his son."

Mr. Grant, and the steel mill, would be in a fierce legal battle for the next year, until eventually an outside company would purchase it. The jobs would stay for the Seven Roads employees, but the name and management would change.

But, at the time, Blake wasn't worried about any of that.

"There are some things you could apologize to me for, Ryan Reed," she said. "But that's not one of them."

He nodded and stood. The story was over, and it was time

for him to leave. He paused though and seemed to become a little sheepish.

"Maybe if it suits you and them, you could send me some pictures and updates about y'all," he said. "I know I won't ever be uncle of the year to the kids, but maybe I can be kind of like a distant uncle who sends them birthday cards and asks after their grades on occasion. Only if it's okay with you though."

Despite herself, Blake agreed. She also surprised herself by hugging the man. His parting words hit deep in her heart.

"Take care of our family, Blake."

She smiled, her eyes starting to water.

"I will."

Ryan seemed satisfied with her answer.

Then he grinned.

"And keep that sheriff around too," he added. "He seems like he'd be one of those really good husbands and dads."

Blake didn't say it then, but she absolutely agreed.

RYAN ENDED UP getting sentenced to several years in prison with the chance of parole. In his first letter home to Blake, he said he accepted the sentence but couldn't deny he was also glad he didn't get more than what he had. Blake wrote back with more or less the same sentiment. She included a picture of them at Clem's preschool graduation and recapped the whole affair, right down to when Bruce squealed for his sister so loud that it started a wave of giggles from the crowd.

The next letter would talk about Bruce starting to run. His first long sprint was the same week that Clem started kindergarten.

Both kids used his new ability to play chase with Liam, but the boy really seemed to enjoy their game the most. He would squeal and laugh, running around the yard full tilt. It was only when Liam had to slow down because of his hip that Bruce would slow down a little too, as if trying to help Liam out. If he wasn't paying attention too closely, however, Clem would run past Liam and catch her brother for him. This became a little game all their own while Lola and Blake usually chatted from the front porch in their chairs, watching.

It was on those chairs one day that Lola finally told them that she had decided to divorce Blake's father.

"We all know that life changes quick," she had said. "In a perfect world, maybe your father and I could have been happy. But life happened, and I think it's better for the both of us that we go on our own paths now. I'm okay and I think he will be too."

Blake had been supportive of whatever Lola wanted but made sure to let Lola know that she could change all she wanted, but her home never would. Lola had laughed.

"Oh, I'm not going anywhere," she had said. "I wouldn't miss this chaos for anything."

Liam had helped her move the rest of her things into the house one day later. Blake's father hadn't been there, something Blake had been worried about. Lola had pulled Liam aside before leaving.

"Don't worry," she'd said. "One day he'll come around and realize how sorry he's been. Until then, all we can do is love Blake hard and love her true. The rest will work itself out."

Liam had liked the advice and thought it was more than easy enough to take. Together he and Lola buckled down on giving Blake love and support until she was finally comfortable enough to talk about her own future. Since she had helped solve quite the scandal and mystery without the help of a badge, they suggested Blake officially end her time off from work and join the McCoy County Sheriff's Department.

Something that garnered a lot of support, mostly from an

unlikely source. Gossip Queen Corrie Daniels was pro-Blake becoming the law again.

"Can you imagine the optics of you working alongside your sheriff boyfriend? I mean, just think about it. You solve a case as a civilian, start dating him, and then y'all are working together on another case and saving each other from bad guys in the nick of time, like in the movies!"

Blake had laughed and so had Corrie's sister, Cassandra. Lola had admitted it would be fun to see Blake even run for sheriff. Price did too. He lightly punched Liam in the shoulder as he laughed while they were all sitting around a table at the coffee shop.

"What if she really did become sheriff? Could you really be okay with that job switch?" he asked.

Liam had laughed.

"Hey, you're not the only one who is a fan of Sheriff Trouble."

By the time Clem's birthday came around, Blake had decided she would in fact start up her law enforcement career again. What position she wanted to apply for, however, was still up in the air. Liam could see even just the talk of it made her happier.

He also bought a ring. Theo helped him pick it out and was mighty proud of it. Despite Liam moving into Blake's house, no one had minded Theo making the guest bedroom his home away from home. He spent several nights a week with them, much to the little ones' delight.

Now he, Lola, and the kids were all inside the house fast asleep. Liam, sitting back in his lawn chair on the front porch, had his hand wrapped around Blake's as both rested on her lap. She was sitting next to him in her own chair, staring out at the rain that had been falling for a few hours.

There were toys scattered around them, a pair of Theo's

shoes by the door, and a glass that had held sweet tea Lola had been drinking but forgot to take in when done in one of the cupholders.

Liam took them all in.

Blake noticed his new attention. She raised her eyebrows. "What is it?" she asked.

Liam smiled. The answer was simple.

"Breadcrumbs."

* * * * *

HARLEQUIN
Reader Service

Enjoyed your book?

Try the perfect subscription for Romance readers and get more great books like this delivered right to your door.

See why over 10+ million readers have tried Harlequin Reader Service.

Start with a Free Welcome Collection with free books and a gift—valued over $20.

Choose any series in print or ebook. See website for details and order today:

TryReaderService.com/subscriptions